THE PASSAGE
OF GALLOWAY

GALEN STEFFEN

The Passage of Galloway © 2020 By Galen Steffen

ISBN: 978-1-7351701-0-7

Book Cover Design & Formatting
by JD&J Design

For the old and the ancient, the archetype and the myth, the beautiful and the fair.

TABLE OF CONTENTS

Part I: The Return

After a great many years of being gone, Galloway, was at last back upon the lands of his home.

Where, from the high hills of the lush forest from which he'd returned, and the rolling slopes of green which sat calmly before him, he began to make his way down into the valley which sat below— down beyond the village built along the banks of the mighty river he went, down beyond the soft groves and the quiet orchards. Down until at last he had reached the grasses of the untamed meadows, vibrant and wild with life, deep in the heart of the vale, and stood before his home: an old cottage which sat amongst the great trees scattered there.

It was a place more dear to his heart than any, but one he had not seen since the days of his youth. For not since boyhood had Galloway been able to return to it.

In a moment that fell beyond the reaches of time, he looked upon this place and the lands on which it sat, recalling in his heart all that had been in the years he'd spent there, and what much there came to be once he'd left it.

Feelings, fantastic and ancient, began to rouse once more within him then— boyish mysticisms and immaculate wonders, impassioned phantasms pining for all that be or may yet come. Things he had not known or felt since the days of his youth were swimming once more within his soul.

How many days and nights I have dreamt of this moment, he thought. How many pulses of my heart, how many breaths drawn through weary lungs have been so only for now. *Can it be that at last it has come?*

Approaching the cottage Galloway stood upon the threshold of its entry and uncoupled the latch before him. Its old wooden door, as if eagerly waiting as long as he, began to fall effortlessly open, and he beheld rooms he had not seen since those early days, spaces that had nearly all but been lost to him.

A great emotion welled within him then and tears began to fill his eyes. For finally: *he was home.* The old boards, long alone and un-treaded, creaked again to life as he stepped inside, echoing out through the stillness of the spaces around, breaking the spell of silence and lifelessness that had fallen there. And drawing in a deep and mighty breath of its air, both utterly familiar, and a half departed ghost of his past, Galloway exhaled shuttering with a long awaited relief. For at last the journey was over.

Making his way about the rooms then he went round and bid unto them a quiet reacquaintance and welcoming; running his fingers along the walls and the furniture, throwing open the windows he let the vibrant morning air flood in; he reset the clock whose counterweights had run out ages ago, and when his heart had satisfied with this process he made his way into the study.

Can I now go forth without first looking back?— he thought as his eyes fell upon the room. For to sail just swiftly by, to be *silent*, and pay not word nor mind, would do me wrong. I cannot now make a trifle of such a treasure as this, nor a single forgotten drop of a peerless torrent, *untold*. If in my haste to live beyond the voyage at my back I forsake the very journey which restored me to it, what praise would this be? For it is a triumph over darkness and shadow, a victory of the soul, and a transformation of the self I stand beyond this day. No, I cannot now go forth without first looking back upon it. *But where is such a tale to begin?*

Galloway unfastened an old and elegantly crafted sword acquired upon his journey and leaned it against the shelf of books. Finding a bottle of ink, he swept the dust from the desk and sat down, producing two more tokens from his travels: a silver pen from his pocket, and an old brown writing book from his satchel. For they had each been instruments of log and ledger to his thoughts and dealings during many the days of his voyage.

Galloway opened the book to its first blank page and uncapped the pen. And as the golden rays of the early day broke through the windowpane before him and filled the room, he placed this pen upon the page and began to write:

How long ago it was, and how much has come to pass, since first I found myself gone from here, old friend. By the measure of my heart it has been a thousand years. By the sun and the earth— *fifteen*. And I know not now where after such turnings to begin. For though the voyage has drawn me far of foot, it has taken me further of soul and self.

It is not now to the home of my boyhood, nor to a mere shelter of the body alone I return at long last— it is back once more to the very *seat of my being*. It is to lands greater than those only of my birthplace or youth, *but this life in its fullest embrace*.

How long the passage thus has been, a thousand years gone from such a place. For in through such time so absent these lands until today, I have found my way upon a single road bent to return to them— one lain by the very labors of that which was dearest to me, *lost*. And conquered at that road's end, an immense valley of the most indomitable of sorrows. I have ascended with mightiest effort unto mountains in my discontent, and then drifted across oceans in everlasting aimlessness.

And where does one begin to say such things that a life has been, my friend? For ah me!— I

have danced among the foothills, a
amongst the forest in my days. I have bathe
the rivers of my love, and sung my praises to the
eternal night sky. I have known both the joys of
giving, and what depletion is reaped from having
given too ceaselessly.

I have known the light of this world, and the
insufferable darkness in its absence. And by the
dichotomy of all things, I have tasted of their
oneness and graced the deepest reaches of myself
along the way.

To learn to live, and thus return home, I have
both lingered long at times, and departed early
from others. Giving the essence of my being over
to both an utter resignation to all things, and an
involvement so pure as to have altered the very
nature of my world and self.

That which has been is no more what now is,
and what I have become is neither fully what I
once was, nor entirely what I had thought myself
to one day *be!*— but is that not the way of it, my
friend?

For though the voyage of this life has been
hard and steep, and taken more from me at times
than ever I knew existed to be lost, to say that for
its hardships it has not been of worth would be a
petty sort of dismissal. Have not the same pains
which have ruined me, had equal hand in making me? And the same burdens that have broken

me, been the very foundations upon which I have learned to build anew?

I am sure that you would tell me now, as you often did, to 'begin at the beginning.' Yet it is strange now to think back to these things that have been— my soul crying for its story to be told— only to realize that the man I have become, who may finally do its telling, is not quite the same person that lived its moments, dear brother.

For I see now through eyes born *amongst* the very feats they would wish look back upon, and *speak* now mostly through words gained *after* the times they would refer to. What bounty there is to be reaped from my days shall be so gathered now with hands that did not sow the seeds. For these hands are not the same which tended those first fragile leaves of their becoming, nor the same which set straight their wayward stocks. These hands are not those which returned daily, bearing water for the roots, casting off the dying parts, or what would not take in this world. These hands were born of that trial, made strong of its burdens, and wise from its failures. For years they toiled in the gardens of my soul.

It is only with such hands made better, *and different*, I now have with which to set pen to page, to voice through what clarities and graces were un-afforded in those yon and younger days.

And still, my friend! *If you would but follow me only one thought further.* What then for
where my journey has taken me that cannot
quite be said? What then for where my soul
has swept beyond this material world and into
realms intangible and unending? That is to say:
w*hat then for where I have encountered the di-
vine?*— For there I find myself at something
of a loss. It seems for everything of the ethers
that has been touched and brought back out
into this earthly place, there will be something
of it lessened along the way. From the direct
unutterable encounter, to even the most intelli-
gible of faithful expression— *for the infinite as
I have known it cannot be claimed.*

It matters not whether by the painter's
brush, or the lines of the poet, not whether
upon the notes of song, or within the quiet
forms of sculpture. For to lend a single shape
to the ever shaping, or a lonely form to the ever
forming, to speak in finite tongue the words of
the infinite, will ever taste of madness to those
who have not first found its flavor on their
own— that which is binding cannot be bound,
that which is infinite cannot be contained, *only
gestured to.* And while it is upon many paths
one may come to knowledge beyond the ges-
tures of this world, there are none who may
walk upon one's for them.

So *if* to begin my friend— *and begin I must*— then aye: I shall begin at the beginning!— of the looking back upon that which did give birth the one so looking, and the saying of such things with words that when first occurred, occurred most lacking, to those encounters which cannot be contained, *only gestured to.*

So *for* beginning then, a final word: the nature of this life we live as such, and the journey through it being what it is— what can thus be said of such a tale and time as this? But that the best which I shall utter of it, *is true*, and yet it is all of it, *a myth?*

Until we speak again.

***

Galloway folded up the old brown book he was writing in, tying it shut with its leather wrap and set it to the side of the desk.

Pausing for a moment he looked out the window before him, watching as the morning light began to envelop the lands of his home in a spectacular golden hew, wrapping up the lush greenery of the meadows and trees in a heavenly sort of luminance. At once revealing only what had already been present before, but simultaneously seemed to imbue it with a quality completely new.

A quiet peace came upon him and he drew a happy sigh for these simple things. For though early yet in the morning: life was abounding; off in the distance tiny figures could already be seen hard at work in the fields of the vale, cutting wheat and corn and gathering them into bushels; while other tiny figures loaded them onto carts and hauled them off for the season's coming festivities.

For it was nearing the end of summer, and the bounty of its reaping was eagerly being collected. Soon the autumnal celebrations would begin, marking a period of time where the labors of the season were rejoiced, and its harvest honored, before settling in for the cold of the long and snowy winter.

Galloway felt an eager pining to rejoin this ordinary but beautiful procession of life. For it was something he had not seen or experienced since last he was home. But knowing at once that there was work to be done first— a bounty of his own to be gathered, he removed a small stack of parchment from the desk drawer and titled it simply: The Passage of Galloway.

Leaning back in his chair he closed his eyes, letting his thoughts carry him off to the days of his youth, and when the moments were right, these thoughts became the stirring of his pen.

***

Part II: The Departure

Imagine for a moment, if you could but recall it,
your first day's love of the sun!—
whose very light had yielded to you: the freedom
of a world unexplored,
and every dream your boundless soul could
achieve within it.
Only to lose that day beyond the horizon;
only for darkness to settle that light.
If boyhood had been my first day's *love of the sun,*
then what followed was surely my first night.

For it was upon such an evening long ago, that I made
my way through the meadows in the valley of my home, out
gathering sticks of wood for the fire's nightly burn.

In the midst of this earthen place sat the simple cottage dwelling of my youth: house of my soul and home of my
boyhood, the very seat of my being it was; a place of warmth
and welcome, quietude and comfort, refuge for both body
and breath.

For there within its gentle walls was kept, a love beyond condition, and a goodness more pure than any I have
ever known. So nestled in the heart of a great valley which

seemed to breathe in endless breaths, what richness this life may bring, and the fullness of its existence, *it was an immensely beautiful place—*

One, where in fall, the autumnal sun would shine, swift and radiant! Casting down its golden rays upon the crimson leaves which danced, more alive than ever, in the pleasant chill of winter's first breath! Or where in spring there burst forth of the once frost laden ground, the irises and wildflowers and charming little tufts of grass, beckoning to all amidst the song bird who'd cry that life has returned, renewed and reborn again. In the warmth of summer days, lasting long into its starry nights, there came the bathing and playing and rejoicing of times in the shimmering turquoise waters of the rivers close by. In the cold of winter, the warmth of carols; in the dead of its nights, the peace of the silver moon. Hot mulled ciders over open flame in fall, pumpkin and cinnamon and every flavor of the season. Books beyond number dwelling in the village close by; knowledge and music and arts of which I hadn't even tasted yet! Indeed, it was a place steeped in the richness of things, where life could drink its deepest breath and thrive.

I thought much of these splendors as I walked through the fields that evening, gathering wood for the fire. What magic there was there! What mystery!— lush forests bordering the lands of the village and my home; mountains rising up gorgeously in the distance, set aglow in fantastic shades of gold and purple from the glory of an evening sun as it descended sweetly beyond the ocean vast, becoming in some other land, the light of the rising! And off beyond the mountains— the great fantastic unknown! Beckoning sweet and silent promises to any who so heard its call. All around me there seemed to be wonders yet untasted, ready to be known.

A boyish grin of a simple love came upon my face and I began to swing one of the sticks I had just picked up. For in the heart of a young boy it effortlessly turned to a kind of dream. With a flick of my wrist the tiny stick became a mighty wand by which great spells were cast!

I imagined that after years of deep study and much devotion, I had become master of a powerful magic, and then traveled about performing good deeds and great works beyond number! I pranced around playfully then, pretending to transfigure one object into another, and as I made my way along, ever upon a quest to find the very best of firewood— I arrived at the base of a grand and gorgeous old tree.

Mightier than any I had come upon before, its towering trunk soared to the heavens and branches outstretched far reaching, forming a canopy so vast, it was at once invigorating and comforting. Pleasantly contained beneath the scope of its reach, I set down what sticks I had gathered so far, and began hunting for more around its base. For it boasted a sizable treasure trove of the many fragments shed throughout its long years.

Eyeing a larger one that would do well atop the kindling, I leaned down and scooped it up with vigor.

Feeling no less playful than before, I quickly imagined it to be an elegant sword I had acquired beyond the perils of a great quest! Gripping it tightly I swung it through the air, dreaming that I had become a valiant knight capable of noble deeds. One who lived for the good, and fought for the right, defending those who could not defend themselves, and riding about upon a magnificent steed!

I swung and thrust this sword about me, leaping and dodging imaginary attacks. I countered and jabbed, ducked and recovered; vanquishing my foes with a nearly flawless form of grace and skill!

Giggling to myself for what fun I was having, I finished collecting a few more sticks of this size and then put them in the pile with the others. Lastly, I began hunting for the largest pieces to become the body of the fire.

As I made my way around the base of the tree— I spotted one! And snatching it up happily, twirled it around for a moment before planting it firmly in the ground. Holding it sturdily with both hands, I imitated an old man I had seen in the village nearby, and began leaning on it like a kind of staff.

What would it be like to have known so many years? I wondered to myself. What were eighty, when I had then only all but ten or twelve? What did it mean to be looking back upon a long life, *well lived?*

My thoughts ran first to the many things I'd glimpsed in my trips to the village— to all the books and art and music I had found dwelling there. For they were things that seemed to hail from every corner of this life, vast and varied, each containing some piece of its wondrous mystery. My days will be filled of them, I thought, drinking them in deeply and coming to know what piece of this life they contain! I shall build a fine collection of great things! Old editions and gorgeous pieces! Beautiful sculptures and handcrafted wares! I will surround myself with them, and be made all the better for it!

My thoughts moved next to the numerous tales I'd heard of people's travels; their adventures in foreign lands and their brushes with danger; the strange landscapes they had come to know, and the histories they had encountered there. For though I had not yet seen it, I knew in my heart what a vast world lay out beyond the valley of my home, and hoped to spend many years off exploring it.

I will set my feet upon other continents, I dreamed. I will walk foreign roads in far off lands, and come to know unfamiliar faces! I will taste their foods and learn of their cultures! I will explore their countrysides, and one day have tales of my own to recount! I will acquire trinkets and keepsakes of my time in these places! Ornaments of the adventure! And I shall make a fine map of the world upon which my sojourns may be marked!

Finally, I thought of the family I might one day have of my own, and the great love I hoped would produce it.

I wondered what it would be like to find someone with whom I could share my most secret of thoughts; a person who is my dearest friend, but also something more. What is it that draws two souls to another, I wondered; alike in ways, yet somehow still in favor through their differences? The thought baffled me, but I hoped one day to have an answer to this question.

Adopting upon my own face the sort of dreamy gaze I had seen on the old man's so often, I stared out into the quiet of the fields, watching as the wind swept the grass into many ever shifting rivers, and saw how the sunlight played upon every blade. One day, I thought to myself, one day I shall make my way to these things.

As the wind slowly stilled, and the grasses once again became calm, I laid this dream atop the bundle of the rest and kept walking. Gathering up only a few more, but as many as my arms could carry, I turned happily round and began the walk back home to build the fire.

***

Dusk was settling now and the fields became even more deeply emerald than they were before. Flocks of birds passed by in the sky above, heading off somewhere to rest, and off in the distance was the gentle murmur of the village settling down for the night. How right all things seemed in the world just then— how perfect and simple and true!

For upon the smallest of things was carried a feeling that seemed to speak of endless blessing: the soft grass beneath my feet; those delicate scents upon the air; what evening light held aloft the sky, and the fire of what wood I had gathered— so soon to come!

"A fine hall, lad!" I heard a voice from behind me shout, and turned to see one of the merchants from the village, waving. I grinned, and he smiled back before kicking the reigns of the horse which drew his cart along home.

Happy with myself for what a bounty I had gathered, I quickened my pace, eager to return home and show my family how much had been gathered for the fire.

Yet as I crested the hill that evening, and the cottage of my home came into view, there arrived something that set a very different course.

For the windows were dim as I approached, which was uncommon at this time of day, and no scents of supper permeated the air around. Yet the lantern out front was lit as it would have usually been. I began to slow my pace as I took these things in, wondering what their explanation was, but could conjure none.

Slowly I moved down the hill, cottage in sight, growing nearer and nearer until at last I had arrived out front, and became certain that something was wrong. For the very air which hung about the cottage seemed to have changed, as though the magnetism amongst it had fled, or its vibrancy been subdued.

Steadily there began to rise, in tones muffled, and words indistinct, the sounds of a most peerless conflict from within it.

I knew neither *what* this conflict was as I stood beyond those walls, nor from *where* it hailed, rather only *that* it was. As I have never known the wind but by the effect it has taken upon all that was around me, so too was it with this.

At once I dropped the bundle of wood I had gathered out front and made way to enter, yet something held me as I tried and I could not bring myself to go in.

For amongst the tones of my family's voices which carried this conflict was something unspeakable; something which sounded like nothing I had ever heard their lips or tongues or beings produce before. It was raw and unsoundly, as though there had suddenly fallen a malady there, one which loomed hideous in the spaces between words, and upon the very tones which carried them.

Again and again I made way to enter from the intent within my soul, yet could not reach my body to move it. Again and again I tried, but was gripped and held and denied rather by some ungodly fear not my own.

I could do not then but stand beyond the walls of that cottage home, that safe dwelling of my simple soul, and listen on in horrified awe.

For minute upon minute it went, growing only deeper and more resolute. I could hear the family I had known to be falling to a ruin of what it had been, and yet there was not that could be done about it. For I could not reach my body to move it, and nor did I know what would have helped if I did.

On and on these sounds proceeded, and regretfully I lingered on only more immobilized as they went. The figures of my family's forms paraded about before me beyond the windows, dim and indistinct in the unlight rooms of this quarrel, until at last, through those tones to which I stood there helplessly listening, something strange occurred. For it was as though the very planes holding time in its rightful place began to bend, and I perceived in awful clarity the years which were to follow—

bows of days would rise and fall like waves upon the restless sea amongst us, never calming, never ceasing, and never knowing lasting resolve. They would rise and fall, and rise and fall, beckoning always of an immanent solution and return to peace, that would not prove to come. For whatever malady that had fallen this night would return, time and time over again, straining and degrading what bonds of love and trust existed, yet would return equally beyond the wreckage of its transgressions, begging the pure forgiveness of open arms. And amongst this horrid phantasm of an unwanted future become, I watched the days come and go for years. I watched as all life became given over to relentless devotions of love, which sought through its goodness to heal, that which was not in its power to. For I would learn amongst those years that the only choices we are capable of making in this life are our own, and that greatly to my soul's lament, it does not matter how *much* there is to be given, if *what* is given is not willing to be received.

So as this strange phantasm played out before me, amongst the discord of that night which wore on —one way or the other— the unseeable affliction which wrought it tore through the fabric that once bound us together, causing the door out the back of the cottage to be thrown open and slammed, and the lantern in front of me to fall to the ground and shatter; whatever bond of love that had bound us as we had been, was broken. And all became an eerie quiet.

**

Stepping back I stumbled over the wood I had gathered which sent me to the ground. Scrambling to my feet I turned round and broke into a run, making for the hills which bordered the lands of my home.

Feeling not my feet which carried me, nor my hands which scratched at the ground as the grade became steep, I fought my way up the hillside until at last I had reached the top, and the woods on the edge of my home came into view.

Breathing heavily I stopped and stared into the forest for a moment, with the evening light of the fading day filtering through the trees before me. I turned round and looked back in disbelief, as if to find some other fate upon this place, or realize it had just been an unfortunate dream.

Yet the lantern of the front door indeed lay broken with its flame extinguished, and off in the distance were the figures of my family, each making their way off to some other place.

As I stood upon that hilltop looking back to see them going, the figures of their forms growing more distant from where they had been, a sorrow mightier than anything I could defend fell upon me. For all that I had known had been bound to that which then ceased to *be*. All that I had wished or dreamt or loved, all that I had thought yet to come, wove its way through a place that was then no more.

The sorrow of this loss and its parting pierced deep into my heart, tameless and without console. It spilled beyond the banks of my immortal self and out into the very flesh of my body, wherefrom it broke beyond my physical form and radiated like sound out into all that I had been connected to— the fields and the meadows, the great trees and the rivers, the streets of the village and the promise of the world beyond, all wept with me.

And as this thing occurred something very peculiar began to happen next: For it was as if in that moment some vital bastion which must never be breeched, had broken, and through it there was permitted entry a host of ungodly hauntings and foes—a thousand figments, vacant and strange, pervasive and unyielding, featureless and veiled in shadow, began to rove and plague upon the lands of my home; praying upon the wounded there and drawing forth from their already compromised condition, the very vital essence of being. The essential vibrancy of life longing beautifully after itself ceased to be. And suddenly nothing became possible. A darkness deeper than the blackest night then fell.

For one dying upon this place became of another, one loss begat a second: as the rivers could no longer bring themselves to flow, the grasses upon their banks wilted and withered and began bleeding into the meadows; in whose absence could no more keep company the trees, that then perished of their loneliness, and in this death did not renew the air, which became stale, and old, and voided of anything breathable. The creatures who drew upon this place for sustenance could not remain but fled, and all the valley became of paleness and perishment; all became desolate and deadened; all became vacancy and void. It was a most unspeakably tremendous kind of loss.

Looking then to my left I saw where the masters of my lands dwelt upon another hilltop nearby, close to where my school had been by the village, and thought at once to seek them for their counsel. But as swiftly as this thought occurred to me, the memory of my visits there were triggered, and I knew it would be of little use.

For I had clambered up their stoney steps many times before this day and joined them in their ceremonies, during which they spoke. Yet ever as they preached those days it became clear they were a people only scarcely aware of the air in which they dwelt, or the soils beneath their feet, or the very world about them. For they harbored only the words of those who had come before them, which they recounted to others, practiced and prepared, but without any true experience or knowledge of their own.

The masters as I found them were able best to brandish the totems of their wisdom tales to others as monuments; idolizing the *pages* upon which they were written, and the *details* with which they were composed, as though these things themselves were the very ideas they existed to convey. And through this baselessness they sought reverie and validation.

Yet it felt to me even then that what truths this life contained were not so flippant or frivolous of things, as to be held in bondage to any group which *claimed possess them*, but were woven rather inexorably into the very fabric of this life as it exists, and the very experiences which define it; accessible in their absolution to any who would so seek uncover and embrace them.

Though in that moment I knew nothing of these truths I thought *might* be, and felt only the overwhelming encumbrance of the loss then before me.

So looking one last time upon the things become of the lands of my home— its unlivable state, and unthinkable occurrence, I turned swiftly round and fled into the deepness of the dark wood.

***

Dank, earthen scents of the forest rose up around me, and I felt a peculiar sort of relief. For this place was empty to me, sprawling out with a blessed, vacant, *unknown*. Traces of the evening light still glowed dimly through the dense coverage ahead, and as I made my way deeper in, the forest itself seemed to swallow the path which had brought me; sealing away where I had entered, that even if I had decided to turn back, I might not have been able to.

For many hours I carried forward pathless in this way, beyond the last light of the day, navigating only by sparse patches of moonlight filtered through the branches above. On and on I went, awaiting a moment that would not come to occur:

For there arrived no fateful encounter here, no fortuitous crossing of paths as the stories read to me in youth would have led me to believe— there was only the solitude of the trees. There was not the gentle fellow, or the learned hermit, no lady of grace to intercept my path and steer me right. There was only the emptiness of the woods.

So I pressed on, knowing not what else cloud be done, until at last overcome by so deep a fatigue of spirit

and soul, that I came upon a small high clearing and collapsed upon the grasses there.

Exhaling a long and painful breath which brought
me slowly to tears, I wept from the depths of my being.
For there was a world now gone to me, an entire existence that was lost; with each good thing and simple
wish born from it, felt to perish with its passing.

Sobbing heavily I turned to my back and gazed
upward. Wherethrough the break in the trees I beheld,
unexpectedly, the immense beauty of the heavens and
night sky— rose reds, and sapphire blues, immaculate
whites shone down with an ethereal light of such quiet
and eternal grace, that they seemed to beckon of a place
far beyond my present state, and instilled, with their
viewing, the subtlest of faint hopes.

The branches of the trees above began to whis-
per in the wind, waving to and fro around this viewing
of the stars, and a strange abandon became my soul, an
almighty resignation in full: to let come whatever might,
let be whatever may, nothingness, or all, *life*, or its un-
timely dissolve.

A pool of water began rising up slowly from the
ground beneath me, enveloping my body entirely, and I
allowed it. Around my legs and torso it rose, covering
my face and moving higher, fragmenting the beams of
light above into a brilliant cascade of the heavens. And
I descended down into this place— deep into a realm of
the innermost did I then quite unwittingly go; beyond all
presumption or preconceived notion; beyond any sense

of worldliness or supposed identity; beyond any intended thing or foreseeable future. To a world within the world did I then become, to a world that is both *within*, and *without*— the self.

As these waters raised higher I could no longer perceive the sky that was above, or the trees which encircled it, but drifted down so deeply that they became obscured from view, and all to which I was aware was that I was being pulled by a great and mighty current.

It whirled me round, spinning and twisting, so that I knew not where up might have been or down *could be*, but carried me deeper, and further, until at last I found my body being tossed in throws of mighty waves, and lost consciousness.

***

I awoke upon the sands of a great beach, lying in the breaking surf of its vast shoreline, which seemed to sprawl out endlessly in either direction. Water trickled from the locks of my hair and the point of my nose as I looked up, beholding the fellows who dwelt there: vagrants and miscreants; beautiful fools and fantastically displaced beings lined the expanse of the shore, which was dotted with innumerable tents and torches. It was as though there was some great festival occurring, strewn about across an endless expanse.

The fellows before me seemed to be constructing an immense heap of driftwood, playfully and without thought of plan, haphazardly heaping logs of every shape and size together in a pile of itself. Laughing and jesting while they did so, swigging from goblets of dark wine filled from a large cask nearby and smoking heartily.

"Who is this mad young savage given up to us by the sea?!" bellowed one amongst them playfully, taking notice of me. "Have you come here for hiding, or to *seek*?!" he said pointing his finger wildly.

"Or has he come here _seeking_ *hiding*?!" piped another, and they all burst into uproarious laughter.

Staggering to my feet, I stood upright and looked upon them, a profound sensation of despair and confusion filling me. For I knew then that I was alone there, amongst this strange host of unintended fellows, and unsought after of new lands.

"Where am I?" I stammered to them with difficulty.

"He wants to know *where he is!*" echoed another playful and amused voice I could not identify.

"Is it really so different from where you were before?!" returned the first who had spoken— though he knew that it was. "You are everywhere and nowhere, young boy! You are amongst everything and nothing. In a space between spaces and a realm of the soul! Neither within your life, or without it; neither amongst the world, nor gone from it! You are where both the lost and the found reside, where both the wayward and the seeking pass through— you are amongst *the deep*!"

I turned round and immediately ran back to the water, hoping that it would carry me back to where I had been, to the world that I remembered, but could not accept was gone.

I threw my fists into the waves as they crashed upon me, each time ejecting me back out and onto the sands of the beach. I stood again and returned once more, beating my fists into the water and yearning it to accept me, but again and again was denied. It sent me only tumbling back unto the shore.

A small black stone washed up in the surf then beside me, and it appeared at once to have been brought from the woods by the same water which carried me.

Picking it up I held it in my hand and could not but become aware of its weight. It was heavier than it should have been for how small it was, both rough and smooth to the touch, and glistened almost mystically when the light caught it right. Reaching down I stowed it in my pocket. For it felt important to me then in a manner I could not explain. It seemed a token of sorts, some single and solitary reminder of what had been, and the things that were lost; the only remnant of where I had come from, or of what my home had been.

"Come, my boy!" said the chief fellow who had spoken first, picking me up and ushering me in. "*Tonight,* we drink and smoke and have beach fire! *Tomorrow—* we regret tonight!" he said with a playful laugh.

The festival welcomed me in then without question, bearing little thought in mind as to what had led me to them, or what the story of my life had been. Only did they harbor excitement for new company come, and a general curiosity as to what made them tick. They had few expectations, if any, of those who arrived. Their one rule, if it can so be called, having never been spoken of or declared aloud by any, was that all who arrived were welcome, and that any who wished to leave could do so whenever they decided. The festival kept no time, no schedule, no routine or habit. They had no boundaries, or borders, or beliefs in particular. It was a place that held no past, nor harbored any kind of conceivable future, but seemed to breathe and boast and live rather, as a kind of inexhaustible entry to infinity unto itself, keeping silent promise that just beyond the next moment into which one might plunge, there would be uncovered some undeniable truth of existence and being, some cathartic rapture through which to be unveiled, all things.

I sat upon a bank of sand behind the fire that first night, looking out to the expanse of shore and sea before me, slowly siping from a goblet of wine one of the fellows had given me.

Twilight was upon this place, wherever it was, and despite my state— the beauty of it could not be denied: a crescent moon hung silent and still out above the placid waters of the sea, casting a gentle reflection of its light down upon it, forming a tender pathway that stretched out to the horizon so pristine, it seemed one could walk upon it. The sky itself moved in ever deepening hews of blue, slowly giving birth to a thousand tiny stars which kept the moon and sea in perfect company, and the air stirred only in the most gentle of warm flurries.

Emptying the goblet of wine and stowing it in the sand for a moment, I looked upward. The shapes the stars were beginning to form above were different than those I knew from the meadows, and this served only to remind me that I was not now where I had been, and that there was no way back, not at least by the way I had come. If the waters of the sea had not informed me of that themselves, I could feel it in my heart: whatever it was that had happened could not be undone; whatever journey, or passage, or descent into a realm of the deep this was, could not be un-started now that it had begun.

"Your goblet grows lonesome!" said the chief fellow, flopping down beside me and putting it back in my hand, replenishing it from a jug he was swigging on.

"What am I supposed to do?" I asked him slowly. "…now that I'm here, what am I supposed to do?"

"You may do whatever you wish!" he replied laughing, slapping me on the knee. "Forget what has been, dear boy. Run wild! *Drink*! *Be mad*! And care not a worry for another's thought of what strangeness may appear. For you will find that all here are no less strange than you— *if not stranger*," he added with a grin. "And it is not so bad a thing to know freedom in madness."

At this he got up and ran down the bank of sand, slopping wine about him as he went, and rejoined the others at the fire, now high ablaze and raging, sending up golden embers into the night sky.

I got up and followed, watching as the fellows paraded about in unorchestrated unity that somehow flowed in perfect accordance with itself. Every step of their dance, every pulse of their play, was born afresh with each new passing moment struck, feeding and building upon itself, constantly evolving into something new.

The chief fellow grabbed a flute and joined the others already drumming, plucking at the strings, and bowing at the fiddles. A spontaneous chant erupted amongst the group and all began dancing in a great circle around the fire.

I watched for some time with obscure wonder and intrigue, my captivation giving way to involvement, the wine beginning to overtake. The melody which stirred the soul in turn gave motion the body, and pushed by one of the fellows from behind— I found myself within the circle. Stirred and moved and pulled onward by some intangible pulse: to clap and croon and dance, to stomp foot and run wild, to smoke the leaf given, and heed no sense of worry for what any other might think. For I held no thought of self then to make any perception either right or wrong, *becoming*, or without favor. But found my soul amongst some freeing thoughtless grace, some wantless being, some breath of the uninhibited, wayfaring, *lost*.

The fire roared with flurries great, and the light itself danced out upon the shimmering waters, illuminated in a turquoise glow from the waves which began crashing and the fellows who splashed and played amongst them. Long into the night did the festival rage, playing and prodding and inciting one another, jesting and joking and breaking beyond any walls one might have held as a barrier.

And I became one of the fellows that night, one of the vagrants and the fools, one of those lost amongst the deep, and I cared not a worry for it. For all that I had known was gone, but there was a wantlessness amongst them; there was an empty peace in the forgetfulness of everything and the expectation of none; there was listless emaciation from any obligating future or encumbering past; there was only thought of *now*.

I grasped a log ablaze at one end from the fire and began parading about with it. Others from the circle soon followed, taking hold of their own, and we marched up and down the beach in wild abandon, chanting our chants and singing what melodies overtook the group, drunkenly swaying and marching on with aimless, fantastic absurdity.

Some began to strip from their garments and swim naked in the light of the moon, others content to drink and smoke upon the still warm sands of the beach did so to the end of their own satisfaction. And as I flopped down beside one of the fellows who was resting upon the shore, the log I dropped from from the fire still smoldering and flickering beside me, I noticed he was clad in the most strange attire.

For the silver chain of his pocket watch glistened immaculately in the firelight, and producing a small leather pouch from the inner jacket pocket of his well woven suit, he began rolling a leaf to be smoked into the most finely crafted cigarette I have ever seen.

"You've picked a fine night for your arrival," he said, as much to the gorgeous expanse of the night-scape as he did to me. "I know most do not inquire, but what brought you here?" he asked with honest interest as he licked the paper of the cigarette closed, lighting it delicately from a match struck upon a rock nearby. Puffing easily on it, he turned and passed it to me, awaiting an answer.

I took the rolled leaf from him and inhaled gently, unsure how to say that the lands of my home and rightful place had fallen into ruin, and that whether it was even possible to return to them or not, I did not know what could be done once I did.

"It's alright," he said, "words come not easily sometimes. They will arrive when they are ready."

"What brought *you* here?" I asked of him in return.

"The poet is no stranger to these shores," he said, referring to himself. "Though not exclusively of course. Yet often have I found myself venturing here, whether by intent or accident, if not for a moment's freedom of what lay *behind* me, then for a moment's embrace of what lay *before* me. There is no better place to be either lost or found, than upon the shores of wild abandon, and unmitigated of impulse."

The poet then removed a small black book from his back pocket and began scribbling something down, presumably words about the thoughts that had just passed between us.

"Don't mind this," he said, "habit or passion, I'm not sure I can tell the difference anymore. I simply write what takes sway upon my mind."

"When did you begin?" I asked, drawing a long inhale of the leaf and passing it back to him.

"I'm not so sure I can remember anymore, to be honest," he said, accepting the cigarette back and drawing on it deeply himself. "When the world so grasped my soul and what feelings I felt within became too great to pass without observance or expression, I suppose... It has been quite some time since the start."

"Did you always know you were a poet?" I asked, receiving the cigarette back.

"If ever I knew anything, it was only that I was *alive*," he responded with a slow and honest exhale, "and perhaps that seemed close enough. For what difference is there between the poet who knows he is alive and thus writes it down, and he who tastes his life quietly, but does nothing about it?"

"Isn't the difference in how you say it?" I asked.

"It may be," said the poet thinking about it for a time. "Or is the difference more in *how* what feelings felt are *known*, that thus bends words to said feelings knowing will?"

Our attention turned toward the figures of the fellows who splashed and frolicked in the waters before us with glee, bare breasted and bodies full born with not a worry or concern.

"You can join them if you wish," he offered politely. "You needn't stay here and converse with me if you do not want."

And though a piece of my soul was inclined, and felt a gentle longing to do so, another part could not have been in more perfect content, than to sit and smoke and talk with the poet upon the shore.

"Perhaps upon some other evening I will," I replied.

And so the waining hours of the night began to pass in effortless ease, with many of the fellows frolicking about amongst the surf in whatever way they wished, and the poet and myself conversing about all manner of great and small things.

***

I took up residence that night in one of the empty tents upon the shore. Though it was nothing but a small enclosure to shelter oneself against the chilly winds which came sometimes at night, and space enough in which to seek refuge against the occasional relentlessness of living perpetually in the moment that *be*.

I composed a simple shrine for myself there, existing of the small black stone which washed up as I arrived, and the threaded fragments of my clothing that began to pull apart as the days went by. I collected also certain feathers and tiny shells from the sea: whatever it was that presented itself to me in moments of deepest yearning or need.

For often in the days I found myself walking along the beach as the others still slept, recounting quietly aloud to myself the things that had been before I arrived, or the thoughts of what might have been if I hadn't. I wound my way through scenarios vast and narrow, wondering if there was more I could have done upon that evening I stood within the meadows, watching as all that I had known came fragmenting apart. And yet only ever did these tiny trinkets arrive to me— eagle feathers blowing gently up the beach as I wept, tiny pieces of my clothing pilling off as I thought the same questions over again, small and beautifully colored shells washing ashore as I contemplated if it all had any meaning or purpose at all.

Each time amongst that place was the same: I would be alone upon the shore in moments of deepest yearning and need, pleading my soul out unto the sea, asking for some guiding hand or answer. And always as I felt that my spirit could not break or burn or want with any greater an asking or more genuine a need, there would follow one of these simple things: the feather of a bird granting me hope of wings, the tiny shell that glistened silently with the promise of better things, or even the wind that would suddenly rage, as I stuck surely upon a new thought, and felt there shift within me, some grand, momentous change.

I would collect and keep what of these things I could, never certain within myself why they should be retained, but also feeling that to ignore them would have been wrong. For how much the less I would be, if after every question asked in this life, only acknowledged the answers that so pleased.

The poet came and went from these shores, fluttering as sweetly into them as he did back out. And in the days and nights that bore his presence, we would drink and smoke and talk to whatever end became; slipping in and out of sadnesses which rose from the things that we had known, meandering aimless into thralls of hilarity found in spontaneous form, and wandering happily into moments of unparalleled kinship; guided then by nothing more than a purely human spirit— to want and know and breathe, to feel and think and uncover, to exist and to be.

As we sat one evening beyond the fire of the fellows, curious to know more of the place I found myself in, I asked the poet how he was able to come and go from the shore so easily.

Looking off quietly to the sea he smoked for a moment before replying quite simply, "I have learned what it existed to teach me, and thus it has no hold on me. We can never truly depart from the things that have not yet taught us what we need to know, my friend. Something brought you here for a reason; it was not by accident you've arrived. And when you have learned what you are here to learn, when you have done what you are here to do, this place will no longer have hold on you either. And you will be able to come and go from it as you wish."

"How long did it take you to learn what you needed to?" I asked him, accepting the cigarette he offered.

"It took what time it needed to take…" he said with a faint smile.

"—More than you wanted it to?" I asked, offering the leaf back.

"Most things do," he said with a sigh. "But the question shouldn't be one of how *long* something will take— it's whether or not it's worth it to take *any* time at all. If something is needed, if something is worth it to be learned or done, what matter is the time? For what lengths of time I've taken and spent doing nothing at all, and indeed, what more will come. Why then should something of value seem like such an insufferable draw?"

"Probably because it's hard," I said.

"Quite right, my friend," replied the poet. "How easy it is to spend great time in waste and nothingness when they are effortless. How much harder to walk any road is when one is counting their every step… But enough of this chatter for now," he said with a smile, his tone lightening. "We have filled our quota of big thoughts for one night, and you will understand what you need to do when the time is right. Let us look next to the sea and the stars, and think on smaller things. And let us also," he said rising unsteadily to his feet, his tone growing increasingly playful, "...replenish our cups from the chief's cask," and grinned.

In times when the poet was absent from the shore I would again rejoin the festival, crooning and parading about with them, setting fires and dancing wildly. But this was not so bad a thing. For as the chief fellow had spoken to me on the night I first arrived, I found myself becoming more and more taken by a kind of madness— one that bound itself to no thought of worry for another's impression, and perhaps even more importantly, to oneself. It simply granted unto the madman the ability to think and feel and do, to run wild and explore, without a lingering sense that whatever it was which occurred, either good or bad, was in some lasting way, *defining*. It was not a madness that struck out against another, or would infringe upon and do wrong; only one which accepted the strangenesses of life it encountered as being something obviously beyond its own creating.

For the madman in me knew without need to convince or assure, that what strangenesses he found were those so bound *to*, and born *of*, life itself. And therefore not within his power to determine or feel responsible for. The madman in me understood that he did not *make life*, or lay its foundation, but realized himself rather to be deeply stepped in the mix of it, a wild wayfaring sojourner born into the experience of *being*. And thus in running wild through it, found nothing but that which was already made to be within it, and felt no shame or worry. For it was neither to his fault nor his credit that the plane of life we all dance upon was as it is, but rather something only to be dove into and known, explored and uncovered, and held in cathartic exultation all the more.

***

The days began to pass to months, and the months to years as I kept count, tracking them with tiny pebbles from the shore: small white stones to mark the days, and then larger grey ones to count the months. I would make a small scratch on the black stone of my arrival as the months turned to years.

Again and again I found myself chasing after this place, by the splendor of the moonlight on the waters of the shore: talking with the poet and celebrating madness with the fellows; smoking his finely rolled cigarettes, and drinking their dark wine. But as the months became years, and the years roved on in aimless unchanging, I began to feel a weariness grow within me.

For eventually there were no more unveilings to be had amongst the fellows; no more great new strange-nesses to tarry off into and forget. There became only a cyclical repetition of all the same— each night a drunken fire to sway too close to; a cask of wine to empty and cast off afloat into the sea, and endless bouts of madness in which to indulge; each eventually bringing only slight variations of all the same.

I began to feel myself a passive participant of these things once bringing me such momentary immersion, playing a kind of routine to myself of the unscripted, unintended, *new*. And though much of what I had known or was taught by the festival was good— wantless and worryless embraces of being, acceptance of what strangenesses became— none of these things returned to me what was lost before I arrived, or helped me to live in genuine peace through its absence. Only did they grant to me a momentary forgetting.

But soon whispers began slowly to stir amongst the fellows in my last year there: quiet utterings of tales about a man who dwelt on the mountain beyond the rising hills after the shore. None of them bearing a complete picture or entire encounter though. For they were tales told and traded only in the second and third hand. Whomever had first begun them no longer dwelt upon the shore to be asked.

Some of the whispers said that the man residing on the mountain beyond was little more than an old hermit, no less lost or alone than any of the fellows, but at least the fellows hadn't given up on things so completely as to never drink or croon or run wild anymore.

Others conflicted with this emphatically, saying that the man was rather some kind of prophet or sage, a great mystic who bore such a knowledge of things that he could affect the forces of nature, and change the properties of matter.

Still some of the whispers maintained that there was no one there at all, and nothing to be found for any who went looking; only a miserable experience without wine or the fire or the fellows, and nothing that could return the time and effort lost in going.

I ignored most of these tales at first, thinking little of them. As it was not uncommon for members of the festival to speak nonsense to one another.

Though slowly as the days of my last year there went by, thoughts of what lay beyond the shore lingered on with ever greater a presence. I could do nothing but hope that there was indeed someone who dwelt upon the mountain beyond, anyone who harbored knowledge or wisdom, or something to teach.

For even if there was no one there and nothing to be found, it was becoming increasingly clear to me that I couldn't stay amongst the fellows forever. All that existed to be learned or gleaned from them had been, and to stay despite knowing this would have been only an act of uncertainty for what lay beyond, and a comfort for the familiarity of the shore I had grown to know so well.

More and more I spent my evenings and nights away from the festival in contemplation of this, talking it over with the poet, or quietly searching within myself for the certainty to depart. I wrestled endlessly about it, wondering if it was nothing more than a vain dream, or an empty, desperate hope.

But as I entered my tent on what would become the last night of my time upon the shore, I knelt down before the small shine I had made and began to pray, casting my fitful thoughts into the air about me.

I did not plea that evening for the immaculate cessation of what burdens I knew, or for their immediate and erroneous release. I did not cry for the swift and effortless return to the meadows I so dearly missed, restored as they once had been. For I knew there was no going back as I had come.

I petitioned rather only for a sign that there was worth yet in carrying forth beyond the shore; that there was something to be uncovered which might either grant me lasting freedom in peace for the things that had been, or the kind of knowledge which could somehow affect them. I yearned only for what things were so needed to change matters for myself— if such matters could so be changed.

At once I saw an image appear in my mind of a man I suspected to be the one rumored to dwell beyond the shore, a figure shrouded in light who stood curiously amongst the stony ruins of some great old structure now overtaken by flowering vines. He plucked tiny pieces of the plants growing there, crushing them between his fingers and inhaling their scents, and he seemed to be at perfect ease within himself.

The image flitted away and as I again became aware of the space of the tent, the small black stone fell from the shrine before me and landed in the sand by my knees— no wind swept round, no shifting of the wooden pillar on which it rested, no motion came to have given it flight, *and yet there it sat.*

I gazed uncertainly upon it for several moments as it laid motionless, glistening in the soft orange glow of the candles illuminating the tent. It could not have been chance that brought it to rest there, I thought, but something else, something which I did not yet understand, but could not equally refute.

I picked up the stone and held it gently in my hand, softly running my thumb across the surface of it, wondering quietly what had happened or how. I thought of every moment in the last three years that similar things had come to occur: the feathers that had found me on the shore or the small shells from the sea, the wind that would suddenly rage as my spirit shifted and changed, and knew that this was not so different a thing. But despite the comfort I had taken in these signs, their explanation still eluded me.

I arrived at no conclusions that evening to give meaning to these happenings, but knew also that I did not yet need to understand— I had received my answer anyway, I had been granted the very thing that was asked for and could not rightly deny it. Despite every breath of uncertainty for these happenings or what I would come to find in leaving, it was decided.

I would go in search of the man upon the mountain.

***

Exiting the tent I walked over and quietly joined the fellows who were gathered around the fire. A most unusual state of calm was upon the group and no music was being played. It was as though they already knew what had just happened, or were at least loosely aware that something was changing.

I took a seat upon a log lain next to the fire and sipped from the goblet awaiting me. A moment of silence passed amongst the group until I spoke. "I'm going in search of the man upon the mountain," I said almost solemnly.

The fire crackled and luminous embers flew up into the air. The eyes of all those gathered round rose to meet mine, and as I found them one by one, I wasn't sure what to say next. I knew only that I had already made the decision within my heart, and that there wasn't any point in not voicing it.

The fellows who believed that the man upon the mountain was real and that there was something to be gained in seeking him, kept as quiet as those who thought it to be a fool's errand. For both could sense that I was going no matter what they might have to say.

"I leave tomorrow at dawn," I said, placing my goblet delicately back in the sand where I had found it, and retired to my tent for the remainder of the evening.

When I awoke the following morning, the night sky was fading to a sun that had not quite broken the horizon, but already there were beginning to gather many of my kin upon the beach. Those fellows whom I had grown closest to in the several years spent upon the shore had come to bid their farewell and impart blessings for the trip.

As the poet approached, he produced a fine leather journal and silver pen from his satchel, handing them over to me with a satchel nearly identical to his own.

"Such things I have found a'dwelling in the midst of my soul," he said, "and all my pleasure to have known them. But how for not they would seem without an instrument, indeed, a wand! by which the sweetness of such spells are cast. Keep log your journey and take pen to your thoughts, and feel not a breath of lonesomeness for wherever this path might lead you, dear friend. As ever may we yet converse when ink from this pen falls upon these pages."

At this he smiled and embraced me warmly, firmly grasping my shoulders before stepping aside.

The chief fellow approached next, grinning slyly, as was his custom, and handed to me the goblet of wine from which I'd drunk in the years previous.

"Take this token and remember us by it! Journey on, dear boy and good friend. We are at home here, but your home lay elsewhere. Find what you seek, become what you must, and keep within in you always what madness you have found amongst these fellows, and these sands! Come see us again some day and regale us with your tales!"

One by one those dearest to me approached to bid their farewell and impart a token of good fortune, or gesture of good will. And after I thanked each and every one of them, wishing them my finest and sharing that last moment of their company, I drew a heavy breath and exhaled, knowing that there was nothing left to do but turn swiftly upon my heel, and set forth to the mountain beyond the shore.

***

The slender path before me rose out curiously from the beach; its gentle, fluid bends twisting off into the foothills like a silent call, beckoning. A silent call which sung of both the promise of better things, and the possibility of none.

I removed the small black stone from my pocket and held it in my hand, wondering if I had made the right choice. But the sight of it alone gave pause to any doubt within my mind, and I pledged myself over silently to a kind of faith that was capable of walking forth consciously into the unknown.

I began then to do the only thing which could be done: slowly place one foot before the other. *Slowly place one foot before the other,* and repeat.

As I climbed the first of the foothills that day I paused and looked back, perceiving clearly the entire expanse of the shore from there. This place that once seemed for so long to stretch out endlessly in either direction was now contained simply in one sweeping field of view: the tents and the torches, the charred sands from where the fires were held, and the casks of wine piled high, all now seemed so small.

At once my heart felt itself to be standing back upon the hilltop overlooking the meadows on the evening I left. My spirit flung itself back to that moment and a terrible sensation of loss overcame me— an echo of the memory from that time.

A frigid shiver crept through me and again the feeling of that day was born anew within myself. I collapsed to me knees beneath its weight and grimaced in the anguish of its pain as though it had been the first time I'd ever felt it. And yet it was not. It was not even the second. It was rather, a time beyond count. For how many moments that evening had returned to me before then was a number greater than any I wished know, and again it had found me somehow born anew, irrefutable and profound.

I thought to myself that it was not too late to turn back— I could still forget whatever this notion was I had in leaving and return to the fellows; I could drown this memory in a cask of wine and forget it in the playful madness which followed.

Yet I thought next of everything else I already knew: that I could not stay there forever, and that there was nothing more to be learned from them even if I went back. Whatever it was that had caused the black stone to fall from the shrine had come only after my yearning for an answer which accepted I would have to leave them. And I could not trespass against that.

I collected myself and rose to my feet, turning away from the viewpoint of the beach and striking forth again to the next of the hills. I gathered up a small staff from the side of the road that was happily a perfect height for me to walk with and found my pace.

I drew long and even breaths into myself as I went, counting each step and though they were a prayer; each breath, a silent petition given up to the way that unfolded before me. Every bend of the road, every twist down the path became a sight upon which I would set my gaze, never deviating until I reached it, to be immediately fixed upon the one that followed.

I ascended the height of the second foothill in the falling light of the first day, soaked in the sweat of its exertion, and began drinking thirstily from the jug of water I had packed: a repurposed jug of wine from the shore.

Most of the jugs, like the casks, were cast out to the sea upon the moment of their emptying. But as I finished this one some weeks earlier, drinking and smoking with the poet, he said something that struck me strangely at the time:

"Ever thought about keeping one of these for something?" he asked, holding the near-empty jug to his eye and looking through it. "Never know when it might again prove useful. After all, only what is emptied can again be filled."

I thought this at first to be only a kind of platitude he would sometimes utter, often in jest for saying such things all too often spoken. Yet as he said it I heard an honesty within him, as though something like this had never before been uttered. And it occurred to me then that every cliche I had ever known, every seemingly trite turn of phrase, was so for a reason. Every platitude I had ever heard had not found its way into being without reason— they were all of them worth something, and only my jadedness for having been ears to them too many times, and too often upon the lips of those I did not like, or when I did not want to hear it, kept me from appreciating many of them for what they really were: beautiful little fragments of wisdom woven into the common speech; tiny tidbits of grace having each been desperately earned; only loosing their relevancy at times by those who spoke them too easily, too thoughtlessly, and too often, and too much without their own experience to substantiate them.

The masters of my lands then came to mind. Had their words been only so much of the same? Beautiful fragments of wisdoms lost upon the tongues of those who hadn't learned their worth for themselves? Or known coherently how to convey them? Reciting them only as matters of the routine or habit they had become so learned in? I didn't have an answer to this, but the thought lingered oddly within me.

Nevertheless, I heeded what the poet had said that night and stowed the empty jug in my tent, knowing not what it would be for until the moment of its usefulness came, and I gathered up my things to depart.

Nearly emptying the jug in what felt to be only a few gulps, I sat in the shade beneath a leafy tree as the sun went down and took a moment to rest. Though only the second of the foothills, the view from it was remarkable, sprawling out textured and vast, with all that my eyes fell upon illuminated by a soft warm glow of golden light.

I rose and, in so doing, made my over to a small stream trickling by and replenished the jug with water from it. I gathered some fruit from a tree nearby and decided to stay the night there. Even if I had wanted to carry forth, the sky was growing dark and I had no reason to continue on without the light. I gathered up my clothes around me to keep warm, using the satchel the poet had given me as a pillow, and began drifting off to sleep beneath the tree.

It felt strange at first not to be in the comfort of the tent I had grown so accustomed to. But as I thought back to it, I realized that for the past few years I had slept only upon a blanket laying in the sand, and how uncommon and foreign that seemed to me at its start was now my accepted habit. How truly different was this tree, or this dirt, or this satchel for a pillow? It was not so very different at all, I realized. Only was it *new*.

I resumed my pilgrimage in the morning, rising at first light and gathering more fruit to sustain me throughout the day. Collecting my walking staff, I set off as the path unfolded before me.

I began to think more earnestly then of what it was I was looking for, and how I would come to find it, the answers for which I yearned, and the man I hoped could provide them.

Yet I had only the vision I received in the tent to guide me, and it offered no actual course. Only that what I had seen seemed to confirm the rumors I had heard: that there was a man dwelling on the mountain beyond the shore. So it was in this general direction I had to go, carrying with me only the hope of what lay at its end.

It could not be said with certainty if I was indeed traveling upon the most appropriate course or not, the swiftest path to the correct part of the mountain. So every now and then I would look to the stone in my pocket as though it might provide me an answer, but of course it could not.

The stone had already told me as much as it could, if it could in fact tell me anything at all, and I could expect nothing further from it. It had given me hope of faith to depart, but it could not make the journey for me.

I carried forth then only by one rule: that I would ascend and ascend and ascend, until either I found what I was looking for, or realized it did not exist to be had.

At which point it occurred to me that I could always return to where I had been— could I not at the very least go back and find the fellows upon the shore? What really was lost in seeking then? I wondered.

For no matter what the outcome was of my pilgrimage, if it proved a fool's errand or something more, there was nothing stopping me from returning. There was nothing to be lost in having gone looking, I realized, only something to be gained. For even if that was only the knowledge that there was nothing there to be found, I could go back to where I came from, wiser and better for having gone searching at all.

A subtle comfort then became me at this thought, a quiet acceptance that I would carry forth to whatever end this path produced, and I would not end before it was done.

The third and final of the foothills before the mountain rose up with ever greater swiftness than those before, becoming increasingly more rugged and rocky in its terrain. The same distance covered upon it felt to be twice the effort of those previous.

Yet every step I took drew me nearer to the top, and every thought that I was closer gave only greater strength to my spirit to continue, a strength I then sapped from my body. But I would not need it soon I assured myself.

For soon I would reach the base of the mountain, and once upon the mountain itself, the man who dwelt there. And surely, at the very least, he would provide me sustenance for having made the journey even if he could not provide me anything else.

I fought my way up the last push of the third foothill and rested for a moment as it leveled off, nourishing myself with the fruit I had picked the morning earlier, and drinking from the jug of water, which I again replenished from the same stream as before, now only further up and somewhat more of a river.

Though day was nearing its end again, and I thought of making camp there for the night, to push on to the top of the mountain in the morning, as I rested for a moment, taking water and nourishment into me, a surge of life flowed through me and I knew that if I gave the final push everything I had, I could make it to the top before the light fell.

Taking one final swig of water and gathering up my things, I composed myself and began the final push to the top of the mountain. Grunting and heaving, breathing heavy in my fatigue and exertion, I tapped every last source I had for strength and plied them unto the path before me.

Nearer and nearer, closer and closer, the peak grew. And I refuted any longing to break, to quit, to turn back, or even to cease for the night and resume at first light of the morning. I fought only on and on and on as the path rose to the top— and I knew that I would reach it. I would reach the summit before night fell, and once there, find the man who dwelt upon it and receive his assistance, I assured myself.

Slowly the top became obscured by the trees and plants which grew upon its slopes. Though as I made my way into them, the path twisted on only upward in its trajectory, and I knew that it would take me to the peak.

Heaving my final breaths and giving the very last sum of energy left within me, I wound my way beyond the final bend in the path, and saw at its end, the break in the low lying plants and trees which meant I had reached the top.

As I circled round and came to the clearing of the peak, I dropped my satchel in the fatigue of my exhaustion and collapsed upon the ground there. Caring not even to fetch a drink of water from the jug, I only panted for some time, slowly stilling the beating of my racing heart, and finding it within myself to rise and locate wherever the man who dwelt there resided.

With great effort I brought myself to my feet and turned round to take in the expanse of the mountain's summit: It was gorgeous in its fashion, covered sporadically with wildflowers and great boulders that rose up ancient in their mass, innumerable and distinct. Vast swatches of its dark soil tore through the rugged landscape of its top, but as I searched round, nowhere were there traces of someone who dwelt there— I saw no stony ruins of some great old structure as I had in the vision, no flowering vines covering it, plucked gently by a man who lived there. Only was there the mountain's open expanse.

I staggered about in my fatigue, searching in vain amongst the boulders as though behind them I might find, somehow, miraculously concealed, the man I then sought and what answers could be known through him. But behind each was only more of the same: spaces of open land, and wildflowers growing about amongst the dark soil.

If there was a man upon the mountain to be found, he did not reside here.

***

I collapsed with my back against one of the great boulders facing the other side of the mountain I had ascended and looked out with soul decimating awe to the expanse that fell before me:

For there stretched out then an immensity I could not possibly traverse, terrains I could not remotely endure or contend with. The mountain I had ascended was not one, *but one of many.* And those which I could now perceive from its top loomed on dispiritingly. For too rough, too jagged, too merciless and bold were they, too shear, and too unassailable. Too many peaks fell before my eyes, and too many possible locations where the man amongst them could reside, if he even existed.

It was not possible, I thought. I had endeavored too great a feat. I could not find the man upon the mountain, whether or not he was even there to be discovered.

I sunk down deep beneath the boulder at my back, crushed beneath the weight of it, which existed only in my heart, and yet I could feel it as though it were directly upon me— I would not find recompense for the things which befell the lands of my home, I thought then. I would not uncover the truth that would unveil their absolution, or reveal a lasting peace to console me in their absence. I would not heal them; I would not return to them; I would not find a way back. Not to the boy I had been, or the dreams he had harbored, or the possibility of all that the world once held. I would neither find a way back, nor would I find solace without them. I would perish there, I felt then, amongst a vast and unforgivingly spired landscape.

And as I thought these things, I realized at once why there was no one left upon the shore to be asked of their encounters with the man upon the mountain—for none of them had ever returned from their venturings to him. Only were there whispers remaining from fools such as myself who had spoken of it before they left, whispers which had then turned to rumors, rumors which then became of tales, and tales that then told of what those who had left had found. But they were only the vain images of hopes conjured beyond want of console, desperate yearnings made manifest in erroneous conviction; hopes which could not accept that good things fail, that honest loves perish, or that there was nothing to be done beyond them.

It had only been fools such as myself who spread these whispers, I thought, watching as the sun began to set upon the vast spine of innumerable mountains before me. It was only those gentle fellows who had found themselves in misfortune upon the shore and could not accept what it was that life had given them. Only had it been fellows such as myself who'd yearned so inertly that such wrong things could again turn right; fellows like myself who began the whispers I then heard as tales, inspired to follow, lead astray by fleeting images given only to myself.

I took the small black stone from my pocket and began to wonder what worth it was. For it had inspired hope to lead me this far, but nothing beyond. Despite its seemingly intentional response to my prayers, it had provided me nothing I could use or learn from. I knew only that it had arrived to me when this journey began, and that it seemed to respond to my yearning to carry it forth. And yet I did not even know *what* this journey was, or *where I was* truly, then. Only that I was lost amongst some realm of the deep, some plane of the innermost, and that I did not know what else could be done.

What kind of a fool hinges their faith on a rock? I scolded myself, holding it out before me and gazing upon it, the rough edges of its shape fitting perfectly into my hand and nearly lobbed it off the edge the mountain in my frustration.

But even in this state I could not help being captivated by something about it, and instead stowed it only back in my pocket, feeling that it would have been wrong to discard it so impulsively.

It seemed that I would die that night upon the mountain, and it would not be untrue to say that I did. For it had required every last fragment of myself to ascend its height, and every last hopeful piece of my soul to believe that upon its top there would be a resolution come, but of course there was not. Only was there more.

And slowly as the sun descended over the expanse beyond I slipped into an imperceivably black sleep; knowing no passing thoughts or dreams that roused to life as the hours of the night waned on. Only did there hum quietly in the darkness some lingering sense that I could not yet turn back; no matter what seemingly impossible terrain existed before me. For the man upon the mountain had neither been found, nor confirmed unreal— only realized to be more difficult to locate than originally conceived.

I swept aside my desperations of the evening before as my thoughts slowly returned to me in the morning, though I felt little the better for it. Perhaps it had been only the whispers of those who'd come before me that led me to be here now, I thought. Or perhaps not. I did not truly know.

Only was I certain that either way, I was where I was, and that I had left seeking something I had not yet confirmed to myself could not actually be found. If I was to turn back from the failure of a fruitless seeking, it would not be so soon, and not still with so many places before me remaining unchecked.

So I gathered myself up and began, not with confidence or excitement for the way ahead, but with the will to persist, I set my feet forth.

***

PART III: THE WAY

For months beyond count I ascended the mountains, and then back down their falling slopes, scaling their sheer and rugged passes, and negotiating the expanses between. Each time I reached the peak of a new one, I would look back to the ones previous and see where I had been, cutting a map of this pathway onto the inside flap of the satchel with one of the rough edges of the stone.

And each time I reached those peaks I was again amazed, not only increasingly by how far I had come, but by that I had done it again. For no peak I ever ascended really became easier, only did I become accustomed to the effort that they each required. And slowly through this process did I come to understand how even the impossible can be achieved.

For the impossible is singular only in the thought which defines it. When in truth, no great task, no unimaginable feat is composed of one thing only, but rather of many, whose complications and requirements will not be known until the time has come to find them, broken down into smaller and more manageable pieces.

From the height of the first mountain, I could not have ascended every, but slowly and surely, from the bases of each, one foot before the other, I could ascend them all. Though with each new peak that revealed it did not harbor what I sought, there came a disappointment and longing, so too did there come glimpses of the things beyond: grand new places to which I would venture, brave new hopes amongst the summits and passes between; each harkening and holding their own blessings of the labors required to meet them.

I subsisted mostly off of what forageings I could gather in those days, which though meek and meager at times, were always ready to be found when I required them most: fresh berries and various fruits, wild tubers and legumes, water from the rivers, and bread won from passing travelers and merchants.

For if my time amongst the fellows had granted me nothing else, it had given me the freedom of madness; a madness which I could use at will to transform myself into a jester of sorts: juggling stones or apples I had gathered along roadsides encountered; playing simple scenes of wild absurdities and witty ridiculousnesses to those who passed by; contorting my voice and character into whatsoever being would illicit a laugh and win me favor enough to be granted a meal.

I plied these skills unto the path itself sometimes; joking my way along that the mountains were not truly as sheer as they seemed, only posturing visages that would yield themselves as I neared; or that the one to which I made my way off next was not really so far, only incredibly small, covering it in the far distance with the shape of my thumb held before one eye.

Though I became accustomed to finding the sustenance I required most when needed, slowly I began to no longer heed concern for whether I would locate it or not as I went along. For increasingly I gave myself up to the way that unfolded before me, and accepted that either I would perish upon it, or be brought to what I sought.

I began a habit in those months of putting to use what gifts the poet had given me: writing the occurrences of the day, and jotting down the noisings of my thoughts. Mostly they took the shape of longings I had, to be back in the company of the fellows I knew well, or memories I missed, musings and questions I wrestled to find my way through. I doubted any of it would make for very good reading, and as I thought this, I became worried the poet would be disappointed in me for not penning grander things, or more gracious words.

But one night as I finished an entry in the moonlight atop the peak of the eleventh mountain, I remembered something he had said to me long before:

"How many thousand scratches I have made upon the page only in pursuit of those fair few that will say simply, and rightly, all that I have struggled to before. And in those fair few marks, I am captured, and I am known. There is nothing quite so sweet as having striven tirelessly to solve a problem, or convey a thought, only to suddenly break upon it, and realize in its solution how simple it was all along."

***

As the twelfth mountain came into view from the peak of the eleventh upon the morning after that night— I stood in quiet amaze.

For the mist that swept round it was something of fable, and it rose gargantuan in its stature beyond the trench like valleys of forest at its feet. It appeared formidable in the very least.

And as I gazed upon it, I broke a silent pact within myself— that I would do whatever it took to ascend its height; I would venture every last fragment of myself to be upon its peak, but if at its summit there was still nothing there, I would go no further. I would accept my losses and return to tell the fellows of what could not be found.

For though I had gained much in the months previous, I could not suffer another unrequited effort. I could not endure another empty yearning and promise-less faith as the ascension of the summits previous had each instilled; all bearing with them a kind of death from longings unfulfilled.

As I descended the height of the eleventh mountain and came to where the base of it met the valley of the twelfth, I began my final embarkment.

I proceeded into one of the trench like valleys of forest at the foot of the mountain before me, following the path as it wound and snaked around through the density of woods that reminded me of those I had ventured into on the lands of my home.

Yet the trees here appeared vastly larger and more ancient, as though they had not so much *experienced* great time, but were the silent keepers of it. The air that flowed round at their bases was rich and cool, imbued with a thousand scents of forest life, made so from the mist that descended slowly from the mountain above, collecting the fragrances as it fell and carrying them to the forest floor.

The light that filtered through their dense canopy was dim and diffused, but sufficient. And where there were breaks enough to allow entire beams of sunlight directly in, it appeared as though great golden spears from the gods had broken through and been lost amongst the shroud of the trees.

I held my hand out passing by one and felt its warmth dance upon my skin, its golden light flashing against my palm. If there was a man upon the mountain to be found, I could not have envisioned a more perfect place to uncover him.

For as I thought back to the mountains and terrains previous, the foothills and valleys between, which though beautiful and varied and vast— all seemed to be lacking something. And walking through this place now, I understood what it was.

For there was breath of an indeterminate magic to be drawn here, a profound intangibility somehow equally as palpable. And as I made my way deeper in, I could only hope that my feelings were not again proved fleeting.

Tiny traces that there were once people who had been there began to loom eerily around: wind chimes made of stone and wood suspended from the lower branches of certain trees, old remnants of cloth banners or tapestries whose fragments yet clung to posts still standing in the ground, though some had toppled over.

I could not be sure that these traces were evidence of what I sought, or the relics of something else. And then a thought occurred to me that had not yet crossed my mind— what if they were evidence of exactly what I sought, but he no longer dwelt there?

How old were the whispers traveling amongst the fellows— real or not? I began to wonder. Years? Decades? More? What if there had once been a man amongst this mountain but he'd died? Or vanished? Or gone elsewhere?

I could conclude nothing from where I was, only that I knew as little then as I had before, and that I would only come to know more if I carried on.

Searching round there appeared no traces of living quarters amongst the things I found; no old huts or structures slowly decaying with the procession of time; no stony ruins in which to find the man or not, and this came as both a comfort and a concern. For I knew not if in venturing further there was more yet to be uncovered.

As the sun began to slip to the far side of the

mountain, the woods and relics about me began to grow imperceivably dark, and I knew I would have to make camp. Though still just past mid day, I could scarcely go further, and the time could be well spent resting and recouping lost energies for the ascent I would begin in the morning.

I nestled into a lovely nook formed amongst the great roots of the ancient trees and a few moss covered boulders which sat timeless in their mass.

I dug into what foragings I had, and then began to pen the occurrences of the day, telling the poet of what faint promise I found in this valley of banners and chimes.

As the waning light grew dim enough that I could no longer perceive the marks I made upon the page, I bound up the journal, stowing it back in my satchel, and retired the pen to my pocket for the remainder of the evening.

Slowly I found myself upon the footings of sleep, with the strange song of the old chimes playing their lullaby in the cool air that fell from the heights of the mountain:

***

I dreamt my way back to the lands of my home as I laid there; to the fields and the meadows; to the grasses and the rivers as they had been before the evening I left. I drew the warmth of their sun upon my skin and felt their winds stir amongst me. I tasted the promise of their days and all they held, beckoning.

Yet at once as I began to find the lasting comfort in their gentle embrace, true solidity of what days so soon would come: they began to rot around me. They withered and died, paled and perished, waned and would not come back.

And I saw my lands as I knew they had become in that moment: a great valley, desolate and unsafe, with what strange figments of shadow that had settled yet roving upon them, still devouring what life fleetingly remained there as it continually sought to renew itself.

I stood upon the hilltop next, overlooking, as I had before in youth. And as I became aware of the dream and where I stood, feeling the sorrowful horror of it untempered, one of the figments took notice and drifted toward me, drawn perhaps to the strongest source of life that was there.

***

I awoke from this dream in the deep of the night with the most profound sense of emptiness that words cannot describe. It felt as though the veil of my soul had been lifted in some unholy way, and all was wane and cold and vacant. All was empty and promise-less.

I felt no shroud between my being and any malignant foe. I felt no benevolent barrier or almighty love-born shield. I felt only the hollowness these beings instilled.

And there, silhouetted by the moonlight filtered from above, stood one beside me: a figure of deepest shadow, stalking.

It felt as though I had become small child with an intruder in their bedroom, standing silent and still beside the safety of their familiar bed.

At first I thought this figure only a relic of the dream just passed, some image my mind could not release and thus transposed it out into the waking world about me. But as I looked upon it, my eyes shifting and fixing upon different pieces of its form: its arms, its legs, the height of its unseeable face— it undoubtedly stood there.

I watched for some time, knowing nothing of what to do, until slowly it shifted from its motionless stance and leaned over me, growing closer and raising its hand near to my face. It felt as though it had come to draw forth from me the very essence of what soul dwelt within; to steal me away and carry me off to a place that would make even the deepest black appear to be bright; where even absolute sorrow would seem a welcomed relief. It felt as though if it took me, there would be nothing left for eternity, as though the most absolutely inviolable place would have been compromised and lost forever. It was the most evil sensation I have ever known.

And yet as it loomed, I became silently aware of something it did not want me to know: that it harbored no power to take *from* me what I would not *permit* it to. It could not absorb what I would not yield. It could not steal what I did not leave open to be had. Its greatest and deepest strength was that it instilled the most godless of fears. But in truth, this was very little— this was not power in and of itself, but the play that my own power meant nothing.

I laid for some time, watching as it waited for me to yield, to be crushed beneath the weight of its profound vacancy, and yet I did not, I only steeled— my soul, my breath, my very being. And looking up to its face, where eyes would have been if it had them, I said quietly to it the only thing that amounted to this in language: "No."

At once it began to recede, recoiling slowly but without immediate dissipation. I shut my eyes against it with the ease of someone drifting peaceably back to sleep, a silent act of defiance, and did not stir again until the morning.

I rested consciously in the quiet catacombs of the mind laced with slumber, abiding this resolution I had never before tasted, and certainly not to such depths, until the morning light broke.

When it did, I looked round to see if this figment yet lingered: behind a tree in the distance, or near to me as it was, but there was nothing. Only were there the morning rays amongst the trees, and the fresh air that roved round.

I wasn't sure what had happened or what I'd done. Only that I had denied it in a fashion. And though I felt safety from the futility I had the night before, I did not feel free of it either. I felt only pardoned, passed, or momentarily spared—

I have to find the man upon the mountain, I thought, *I have to find one who can account for this to me.* And slowly it began to make sense to me: that if something as depraved and vacant could not only exist, but take such substantial effect as these shadows, then surely something, or *someone,* dwelt upon the other side of the spectrum to lend equal countenance. And if I could know one, then I could know the other, and if I could be affected and found by one, then I could be affected by and, in turn, *find* the other.

There had to be a man upon the mountain, I concluded. There had to be one who dwelt on the other side of things, or could at least impart lasting guidance and imprint as to what that other side was, and *I had to find him.*

There was no going back now, no return to the fellows and no notion of life without. There was only an answer to this, or nothing. There was no other way.

I picked up and carried on as the path went forth, twisting its way deeper into and through what would either prove to become the shroud of a hapless seeking, or the very woods which lent balance to its unveiling.

***

Beyond the valley of the banners and chimes I began my ascent. Up, up, and up I went, thinking nothing of what effort it required me to do so on this greatest yet mountain of the journey. For my thoughts were focused only on what I would find upon its top.

I wound on for hours and hours the first day, following the switch backs as they carried me in places to slender corridors of the steepest and most rocky terrain, and then to the most narrow of pass-ways which hugged tightly the walls of cliff sides plummeting too far below for the eye to see the bottom of. Back and forth, up and up the path went, weaving and turning and seeming to carry me all across the mountain as it steered its way on and on to the top.

Some three days of this persisted, until at last upon the third I became certain I had passed the same rock formation several times, and was thus going in circles. First I had passed it in the morning, then again midday, and now once more as the light was beginning to fall. And yet there was no other way the path could have gone. For immediately upon my left rose up an immensely sheer face of rock, made slick and unclimbable from the mist and moss which grew upon it, and to my right, only another cliffside plummeting down.

I stopped and set down my satchel to examine the rock formation. It had a most curious composition in that, if viewed only from the angle of approach, it was in no way remarkable. But to turn ones head toward it as you passed by revealed, if only for the most fleeting instant, the image of two figures holding between them, a chalice or cup. To take even another step forth was too much, it was fragments of a step rather, indescribable divisions of a singular thing that revealed something which could have otherwise gone so easily unnoticed or missed.

And yet there it was, again and again as I repeated the process, perceivable only with the greatest of precision. It required such a delicateness of motion that it took me a great many attempts to find exactly where the image appeared and where it did not, slowly isolating the movements of my body as I stood before it, until at last it was only the most infinitesimal motion of my head to one side— *before the image itself became locked in.*

At once a group of ravens flew beyond me in the sky above cawing, the feather of one breaking free and beginning to float down, carried upon wafts of wind that brought it precisely to my hand as I outstretched it before my face.

Within my field of vision the feather now took the place of the cup the two figures had been holding, and slowly, ever so slowly as I lowered it, there was revealed an opening between them, with a slender stony staircase rising up to somewhere, and a glowing lantern hung upon a nail in the rock of the wall at the bottom of it.

I gathered up my satchel and stowed the feather inside, collecting my staff and the lantern from the wall as I proceeded slowly up the stairs to wherever they might lead. Step by step, foot before foot I went, wondering silently what awaited at their top.

So long did the stairs stretch on for that I thought in moments I might become trapped within them. For to look the way down revealed only faint light cast from the lantern until it dissolved slowly into darkness. The way up, the same.

I cannot say how long it was I ascended the stairs. For several times I rested upon them before reaching the top, the lantern never extinguishing, and the rations I had gathered days earlier seeming to sustain me longer than they should have. But finally after what might have been a day of this climb, I came to their end, and reached what was there to be found.

The last of the stairs grew increasingly shrouded by various dirt laden roots protruding from the walls and ceiling of the rock they had been carved into, and as I emerged from them it was most nearly from the ground, as though I had been coming out of an immense grotto or cave, encompassed at its end by a large stone archway, and all manner of rich plant life. I stood then upon what appeared to be the top of the twelfth mountain.

Around me there was immediately visible the remains of things similar to those I had seen in the vision: old columns scattered about and crumbling, fragments of what appeared to have once been walls of structures whose purpose was unknown to me now overtaken by a variety of flowering vines, and certain areas that might once have served as places of gathering, long unused, appeared upon my left.

As I made my way further into the ruins I kept the lantern close about me. For though it was twilight when I had emerged from the grotto of the stairs, it was dim enough to still feel aided by its light, and comforted somewhat, as I had grown accustomed to it being in my company by then.

In the distance beyond the ruins first apparent to me, down the twisting stoney path overtaken with grass which snaked its way through more crumbling structures, I could see a single flicking light. Perhaps a torch or fire, I thought. For it was too large to have been a lantern alone.

I began making my way toward it, wondering what it would reveal. Was this the man upon the mountain I had sought now for so long? Or yet another promising thing ultimately proving disappointment?

Slowly as I approached, the light grew larger and clearer, finally taking the shape of a small fire with a single figure seated behind it, gazing into its glowing flames and gently breathing the scents of something it held in its hands. Was this him? I wondered to myself again. *It had to be*, I thought next.

For behind the figure stood the silhouette of the only structure remaining intact I had seen. It appeared to be a small house or dwelling, adjacent to the center of the ruins, and near to a large area of lush plant life, perhaps a garden.

As I neared closer and closer, clearer and clearer the figure grew, until at last I became certain of what it was, and came to stand only a few feet away. The light cast from the lantern now mingling with the glow of the fire— the figure spoke. "Greetings," he said softly, raising his gaze to meet mine, "you've arrived."

I had found the man upon the mountain.

***

For a moment only the fire crackled and sparked between us as I slowly took in the gravity of what I had finally reached, and the man who sat before me. So long had I been in almost ceaseless pursuit of this place that as I finally stood upon it, I realized I had no idea what to do next.

It was strange to perceive with my own eyes the images of what had only echoed in my memory so long. The vision by which I had first glimpsed them feeling almost lifetimes earlier. And despite the fever with which I had set forth from the valley below, the certainty I felt that there existed, somewhere, what I now stood before— to be there at last was unspeakable surreal.

For it occurred to me then that not in all the time spent looking did I ever truly imagine myself to reach it. I had never thought of what the first exchange with the man upon the mountain would be, what he might look like or say, or how I would come to phrase what questions needed asking. I had not pondered the nature of what the experience would be if I reached him. I had only fought to not give up the hunt, that there was either something to be found, or not.

And though all which now appeared before me was nearly identical to what I had glimpsed in the vision, as I looked upon the man seated behind the fire and gradually became acquainted with his presence, it occurred to me that I could not tell his age. I knew not whether this was important, but it was curious all the same.

For he appeared as though upon the cusp of what vibrancy spurns from youth, but also bore the marks of things that come with time: fleeting traces of silver peppering his hair and beard, small lines and marks upon his face from what the years had held. Though still, he seemed entirely upon the greatest becoming of what any life could hold, silent and strong and effortlessly composed.

"You were expecting me?" I asked finally, my thoughts at last catching up to the present.

"I await any who arrive," he responded slowly and succinctly.

"What was this place?" I asked, looking around.

"This place?" he said, following my gaze to the ruins about us. "For time beyond time this was a place where kings had trained, where those who had gone seeking the truths of things that *be*, came to uncover them."

"What happened to it?" I asked.

"Kings do not come anymore," he said simply.

"Why not?" I continued.

"There are few kings left, it seems," he said almost sadly, his gaze falling to the fire and the remains of the plants he held in his hands.

"Were there many before?" I asked.

"Oh yes," he responded slowly, his tone shifting. "Once upon a time this place was teeming, not only with the kings who had sought it out, but those who dwelt here teaching them. Once upon a night such as this, the torches of the columns just there would have been lit," he said gesturing to the gathering place I passed on the way in, "and all would have assembled as we did each new moon, to trade words of thoughts and lessons that had been since the last. It was a fitting way to mark the passing of days and the fruits of one's labors; with each new phase harkening a new chapter of work and discovery."

"Were you the master of this place?" I asked, wondering why it was only he who was left now.

"—The master of this place?" he returned curiously. I nodded.

"What greater master of a place could there be than what truths it holds to be known? That was the spirit on this mount then, and remains so to this day, and all who once dwelt here teaching knew not but such things."

"What things?" I asked.

"Things which guide the way. It is not to say that we knew all that had been or would ever be, not of all things in all times. For that is omniscience or trivia, not wisdom. Wisdom is that which steers the soul, dear boy.

Wisdom is the difference between information and truth. I have encountered a great many who have come here seeking, deeply learned in every manner of subject: histories and sciences, arts and the like, and yet had no idea *how* to live, or *what with* their knowledge to do. For they knew nothing of the truths that be.

And while each who once dwelt here teaching had fields of their own study, for some the cosmos, others the cards and prophecy, healing and herbs as mine had been, there were none who possessed wisdoms the others did not. In all things guiding a being to a place of greater truth, we were equals. And in company of those who know not but the way which leads to greater things, there is no need for a reigning master. When one has learned to see, and knows that to which to listen, all things become singular and one. To have learned from any, was therefore in a fashion, to have learned from every. For one could not point the way better than any other."

"What happened to them…" I asked, "…to the others who taught here?"

At this the man drew a great sigh and again gazed down to the fire. "All things must come to an end," he said with a tone of sorrow. "Slowly the others departed from here. For gradually the kings came less and less, and as the years began to pass with none but the teachers remaining and no one to be taught, eventually they did not stay either."

"Where did they go?" I asked.

"To the far seas of what lay beyond," he said, "to the journey that is next," gesturing to the other side of the mountain that held a vast sea beyond it. "Across the sea and beyond the setting sun, to what realm exists after this one."

"Why did you not go with them?" I pressed. And at this he paused, choosing his next words carefully.

"My time was not yet finished," he said, thinking for a moment, "I could not have explained on the day of my remaining how I knew I should have stayed or not. For many of the others had concluded that the time of the kings was done, that the age had passed, and those who were unsure eventually followed anyway... but I felt a lingering uncertainty. It was, I think, the only disagreement we ever had amongst ourselves that could not be reconciled in discourse. So alas I stayed, feeling only that I had not yet done all that I was here to do, and that there had not yet come all who arrive seeking. I have spent the time since in practice and study, awaiting any who would next arrive."

"How long ago did they leave" I asked, silently contemplating the state of the crumbling structures around us.

"A great many more years than you would believe. For time does not pass amongst this mount same as it does where you are from" he said. "But I have not remained here for count of years, rather only for those who would come seeking still. There is much left yet to be taught."

"But I am no king," I said, wondering what right I had in being there at all now that I knew what it was.

"Perhaps not," he replied, "or maybe still— that has yet to be seen. What can be said with certainty is that you have arrived here all the same, and only the worthy are able to do so. Thus you are worthy to be taught.

"But why am I worthy only for having arrived?" I asked.

"Surely you must know by now, my boy," he said taken somewhat aback by what I then still did not fully comprehend. "Only by the signs would you have come to find this place, and only are the signs given over to those who seek, and only worthy seekers are able to read them. I do not yet know what your way has been or what has led you to me— *why* you have come here seeking or *what for*, but only those willing to find what *is*, and not solely what they *wish to be* would have been able to arrive here. Do you know how many have this far ventured, only to at the final moment give up for having failed to perceive the image which revealed the stairs to you? Most continue searching only for what they have determined the path *should* be, not permitting what *is* to unveil itself. They think the path should wrap round the mountain and continue on up, as that is the nature of all other paths they have walked before, but when it does not proceed that way and they fail to locate what they seek, they give up, concluding erroneously that it never existed to begin with. It is a curious case, my boy, that when seeking what we have never before encountered, we often do so in the same fashion as all else we have ever found. But why should the path to what is new be the same as the path which brought you to all else that came before it?"

"But I did *want* to reach this place," I said after thinking about it for a time. "I saw it in a vision before I left the shore, that's why I came."

"As did all who ever came seeking it. But was not this vision one of the signs of which I spoke? For the vision would not have come to you if your soul had not first stirred to go beyond where it was, and you would not have come to realize this vision if you had not left further seeking. For tell me— despite what faith you may have placed within in it, was this vision alone a map of the way to *what* it showed? Or even the certainty that what it showed, *existed?* Or was it rather only a glimpse enough, of a *possible* point you knew not the course to reach, that lead you looking for something better? This moment now is not a moment of having found what you *intended* to find, my boy, but of having found what you *hoped* to. And that, *that*, is the difference of worlds.

For to venture forth and seek beyond the comforts of the familiar that which lay amongst the unknown is an act requiring the deepest of faith, and yet curiously it is only by this spirit one is lead to the greatest of truths to be *known*. For only by that effort will you ever come to find what *is*. You may count yourself amongst the fair and few then, dear—?"

"—Galloway," I said.

"Dear Galloway," he continued. "It is no simple or easy thing you have now done, and it is not for nothing I said it was kings who had once trained here."

I could do nothing then but hear his words and hope them to be true. "What do we do now?" I asked. "What is the next step?"

"The next step, dear boy, is a cup of tea, a good meal, and a rest. For you cannot unveil all things in a moment. They will take time, time and persistence. The real training shall begin on the morrow."

"Wait," I said, stopping him as he rose from the fire, "I have a question about the signs. I know you said they come to those who seek, and that only worthy seekers can read them, but why do they even come at all?"

The man looked upon me in silence for a moment and then spoke, "should it be so strange or impossible a thing, my boy, to in this life be both the affected, *and the affecting?* That as we are in part shaped by the world in which we find ourselves, it is only by the shape so taken, we make it what it is? You are born *of*, and bound *to*, all that be my young friend, both affecting and affected, both determining and determined. What signs have come to you have done so for what you first cast out to the world about you, and the world is listening. As you called to it in the silent nature of your soul, it responded in what ways it could— by the birds and the air, by the sea and the wind, by whatever manner of its things would speak to you. For that is the voice with which it has to communicate, and you will find that it will guide you in your way if you only allow it.

To be young, dear boy, is to hold within you all the power you will ever need, and yet know nothing of it. You have magic within you, young Galloway, and things are far more than you yet know."

The words echoed round in my mind after he spoke them— that as we are in part shaped by the world in which we find ourselves, it is only by the shape so taken we make it what it is. And I could not help but to think of the lands of my home.

"But how does one change their shape?" I asked. "How does one change their shape so as to take what affect they wish?"

"Ah!" he said. "There it is! The *why* after which you seek— you cannot change your shape, and thereby cast what affect you want, if you cannot first wield your mind. So that is where we shall begin. You must become a master of your thoughts."

Silently I nodded to him, still stewing about what had been said.

"So then," he continued, beginning to gather some fresh herbs which grew amongst the perimeter of his dwelling, "come with me to the kitchen and I'll make us dinner and a cup of tea, and you can tell me the tale of what lead you to be here… And have a smell of this," he said, handing me a small flower plucked from the vines growing upon the ruins near. "They have a most remarkable scent."

***

Over dinner and tea I told the man upon the mountain the tale of my days, and he listened intently, interjecting only in certain moments so that I might provide him with greater clarity I failed to at first.

"You cannot change the things that have been, my boy," he began slowly as I finished my telling, "only affect what comes next to be. And well on the way to that are you already. What must be done now is to arm you with what weapons you will need for the fight ahead."

"The fight ahead?" I asked.

"The figments you spoke of," he continued, "the ones veiled in shadow. They are no minor foes to be trifled with or known. And the path of your days is bound inexorably to an outcome with them. For you cannot change the occurrence of having known them now that you have, only respond in kind to the effect of its happening. And your options are one of three:

—You may either accept their presence and nature, find a way back to the lands of your home and live in it as it has become, something which if you could have done, you would not have fled from it to begin with.

—Or you may depart from what you cannot accept, thereby removing it from your life. But you have done this already, and if it was a solution for you, you would still be with the fellows upon the shore. Not to mention of course that these figments haunt you even after having left."

"And the last?" I asked.

—"You may change it," he said. "That which we can neither accept as it is, nor remove from our lives, we must change. There are no other options than these, no other responses which can be taken. Therefore you face an inexorable encounter with these figments, a confrontation which will determine not only what becomes of the lands of your home, but the very fate and nature of your life and soul."

For a moment I only sat across from him at the table, silent and pensive, as I slowly processed what he'd said.

"For what it's worth," he continued, "I'm sorry that you find yourself in this place, there are certainly happier tales of those who once came here seeking. But take comfort in knowing that while the things which happen *to us* in this life may at times be awful or unfair, they are far less important than the things *we do* in response to their happening. For that is the true place where your life is determined. We cannot always control what happens to us, my boy, but we can always decide what we do next."

I nodded to him slowly in understanding. "What are they?" I asked.

"The shadows?" he replied. I nodded again. "They are not actually shadows," he said, "not truly. For a shadow is what is cast by a living being, or anything actually present in the world, and these figments are neither. But I'm sure in a way you knew that already, having been in their presence and experienced what effect they take. They are, put simply as I can, fragments of the darkness— where fear and emptiness have found form, and sowers of the very seeds which reap evil; they are a rot at the heart of love, and good things otherwise pure, endeavoring only to steer one's soul adrift from its proper course, and therefore cast darkness in the world where there ought be light."

The words seemed to confirm the feelings I had felt in their company. "But if they are not of this world then where are they from?" I asked, attempting to process everything the man had said to me.

"There are none who actually know, my boy. For that is a journey to a place none wish make, and I'm inclined to say, even *if* made could not be returned from. The best thought is that they hail from some other space, a realm that exists in parallel to ours but typically separate. A place of profound vacancy and insatiable hunger. They seem to in some way be nourished by drawing upon what exists in our world and taking the souls of those who surrender to them back to wherever it is they hail from."

"But if their world exists in parallel to ours then how did they get in?" I asked. "Something that's parallel is still separate, isn't it?"

"It would seem that such things find entry through spaces of a kind of fatigue," he said, "when love is made wane, and goodness, diminished. As though an intangible bridge were formed, or a veil pierced, when the conditions that define their world, are mirrored within our own."

My eyes began searching back and forth upon the table before me, my mind grappling and processing the information which all seemed to ring true.

"But why me?" was all I could conjure to to say or ask.

"I would venture," the man continued, his tone softening, "that when you experienced the loss you did, it struck to the deepest parts of you, and so bound to the world around you, you unwittingly took this effect upon it; weakening it in kind. And by that rift or bridge so made, they were permitted entry. The question of 'why you' is largely answered in this, but there is also something more. For there are few of whom I am aware who have ever actually *seen* these beings in their full form. Most only discern the intangible unsavoriness of their effect, and while we are all in part shaping the world that is around us, there are few I have known capable of doing so with such totality as you described."

"I'm sorry but what does that mean?" I stammered to him somewhat, unable to assemble the pieces he had laid out before me.

"It means that you had more of what they want than most, my boy, that is why they came for you. And that is why they will continue to occupy your lands unless driven out. It means that you had been more filled with the kind of life they so crave, more inherently bound to and effortlessly becoming of all that you encounter than most, and therefore a richer target to be stolen from; a more effective conduit, if you will, of the things to which they are drawn. So much so it seems that they did not mind being seen by you. For their nature is largely to remain hidden, pervasive and persistent, whispering from the shadows."

"Whispering from the shadows..." I said aloud thinking, as something began slowly to make sense. "...a rot at the heart of love and good things..."

At once my thoughts swept to my family and what strange malady seemed so swiftly to have fallen upon it, how it hung in the spaces between words and seemed to in some way be guiding them.

"—My family..." I said, raising my head to the man, "they were what...?" At this he only nodded silently, knowingly.

"We are each the keys to the lands of our own homes, my boy. You were what could permit these shadows entry to the richness that was there. But only if you were weakened enough to do so first. It is a most unfair thing that occurred. I will not say to you now that you face impossible odds, though they may seem as such. For you have learned in making the journey here that even the impossible can be overcome. And though these figments which plague your home will haunt you for all your days unless driven out, in their carelessness of being seen by you they have also given you a hidden gift— certainty. For you know now the enemy far better than most ever have or will. And though it does not lessen the pain of what they have taken from you, it is no small thing to know what you face. For in knowing what one faces, one is better equipped to confront it."

"You said I was one of the few who had ever seen them. Who else has?" I asked the man.

"There are only two of whom I know with certainty," he responded. "Both of whose time was much before your own. But there may be others."

At this he rose from the table and made his way over to a voluminous bookshelf, containing upon it what appeared to be innumerable tomes telling of a vast array of subjects. Scouring the shelves for a moment, he ran his finger upon a number of spines before locating the one he searched for. "Ah," he said, "here it is."

Making his way back to the table he set it down with a great thud and threw it open, hunting for the proper page. Flipping through it for a moment or two, he found the page for which he searched and spun the book around so I could see.

"Here," he said, pointing to a kind of sketching, "this."

There appeared before me then an identical rendering of the figures I had seen— shadows, slender and featureless, leering from the dark.

"Where did this book come from?" I asked eagerly.

"It was written by a holy man," he said, "not far from the lands of your home actually, but much before your own time. It was his autobiography, and where much of my knowledge on the subject comes from, beyond of course what darkness I have encountered in my own days. There is little more he says about these beings than what I have already told you. One of the most notable entries concerning them was that, 'one appeared to him one night,' and that 'he knew it had come for his soul.' Unfortunately for us, but perhaps happily for him, that was the only time they ever visited him, at least in their full form. His next entires go on only to tell the latter occurrences of his life, which I'm sorry to say, will prove most unhelpful to you in this matter."

"And who was the second you've known whose seen them?" I asked.

"The second was actually one who once ventured here," he replied. "A seeker of the things that be, not unlike yourself. But again, the occurrence of his knowledge about these beings was cursory, only a brief encounter with them had he had. Something which came up one evening as we traded tales about our lives. Neither of the two I know of were remotely as affected by them as you."

"So what does that mean?" I asked the man, growing frustrated, unsure of what value could be drawn from this information.

"It means that something very different is happening here," he said, "something different than ever seems to have happened before."

"How can you know that?" I asked.

"Quite simply," he replied, "if what you are now enduring had occurred before and been surpassed by another— would you not already know about it? For can you imagine having gone beyond what you now face, having conquered and moved passed, only to never speak of it to anyone?"

I thought about the question for a moment and the answer was obvious.

"No," I said. "No, I can't. How could I not tell others of this if I came to its end?"

"You have denied one of them once," he continued. "You have tasted the essence of what you will need master to rid them from your home, so we are not lost completely. But you will need to come far, and grow strong, if you are to face the others which remain. I will teach you what I can to aid you in this."

I nodded in agreement and he continued.

"But there is something else that tells me this is different," he said. "…The stone you carry."

I removed the small black stone from my pocket and held it flat in the palm of my hand. "It washed up when I arrived," I said. "It came from the woods beyond the lands of my home."

Slowly the man shook his head 'no'. "That stone did not come from the woods you were in before the water brought you here," he said. "It came, rather, from this very place you are now making your way through, and it comes in fact, to very few."

"What do you mean?" I asked him. "What is it?"

At this his eyes only gleamed, and he sparked the faintest of smiles.

"It is difficult in a word to surmise," he responded. "It is not some simple totem you now carry. It is something much more. But perhaps that is knowledge best saved for another day. Trust me in that you will know what it is when the time is ready," he said. "For now, we have spent enough time in discourse. You need rest— take rest. And we shall continue on the morrow when you are well enough to do so."

***

Beyond the following morning in which I slept late, the man would rise each day at first light and wake me to begin training. We would meet always in the same place: a large open area of circular stone.

"To master your thoughts you will first need learn to focus your mind," he said the first morning we met there. "Once you have learned this, you will be able to explore and know your thoughts for all they are, and find yourself seated in the intangible space where thought becomes being, *being* becomes self, and self becomes of all you make around you. To learn to focus the mind we will begin with these," he said, producing an ancient and beautifully crafted sword from its sheath, offering it over to me. Drawing his own, he laid the sheaths down at the edge of the circle and began making his way back.

"These belonged to one who once taught here," he said. "She found them to be a most useful tool in the effort of focus, and quite gifted with them was she as well. Never once did I see her bested in all the time we dwelt here together. And certainly not by me— though I did come close once," he added with the small grin of a fond memory, "I learned much from her."

"She?" I inquired, interested to know more.

"Indeed," he said, inclining his head to me. "One of the wisest and most ferociously spirited women I have ever known. She was graceful as you've never seen, and strong in every way that matters most. It is much to the misfortune of this place that she no longer dwells here."

A quiet sadness then became visible in his eyes, seeming to speak that there was more there to be known than he'd yet said. Though I did not in that moment ask.

"That dwelling up there was hers," he said, gesturing to a small, single roomed hut on the highest point of the mountain top. "It is where these swords are kept and to where you shall return them each day when we are done," he said, his tone shifting, indicating that this was a subject about which he had no more to say.

"I understand," I said. "I will."

"Good," he replied. "Then we shall begin."

The man began walking the perimeter of the stone circle, swinging the sword in his hand and coming to know its weight. I observed and followed in kind.

"You will need to master the focus of presence which enables you to dwell, in a sense, in all times at once. The past, for what previous lessons and knowledges you've gained, the present, to perceive where these things need be applied, and the future for anticipating where the present might lead you, and what counter attacks or tactics you'll launch in return. To speak it aloud sounds cluttered and confusing, to experience it within feels silent and still. For once mastered, it will cease to be a conscious process of your thoughts, but a thing which flows through you rather, seamless and unobstructed."

At this one of his gentle swings to feel the weight of sword formed effortlessly into a masterful cut which brought the edge of the blade to my neck.

"Be alert," he said, "silent and aware. One moment may turn to any other in a breath."

He withdrew the blade from my neck and made a few paces of distance between us, still circling.

"Let not your failings or mistakes of past define your thoughts of it. Know them for what they are, but rather than becoming your shackles which bind, find them as the keys which unlock the future."

At this he swung again, and I parried, catching his blade as it made its way again for my neck.

"Good," he said, as we held the stance, blades locked together. "That was the past coming to serve the present. Now what of the present coming to make the future?"

At this I pushed back against his blade and the weight upon it, swinging for his torso once free. He deflected and countered the attack easily, slowly returning a blow meant for my arm. Again I caught his blade, and again returned an attack. He deflected it another time with ease and forced me off balance.

"Good," he said again, "*good.* In time you will learn to keep yourself centered no matter what attacks come your way. With your feet beneath you and your weight close, you will not so easily lose balance."

Pausing for a moment he allowed me to breathe and reset myself. "You will find in the course of this practice that not only will it strengthen your ability to focus and wield your mind, but through it, your body. And both are of great value."

Drawing one final breath and releasing it slowly, I had calmed the beating of my racing heart and refocused my mind for the next bout.

"Again." he said, once I had readied. And so the morning continued.

***

After some hours of this practice the man stopped. "You have done well today. Go and return these to their proper place and meet me back here to continue training," he said, handing his sword over to me.

I gathered up the sheaths, stowing the swords inside, and began making my way up the slender pathway to the small hut which sat at its end. From the elevation I gained on the way, the entire expanse of the mountain top became revealed in gorgeous panorama: from the grotto of the stairs, to the gathering place and its columns, to the training circle and structures which sat crumbling, to the dwelling of the man, and the gardens beyond, all entwined by the flowering vines which grew there. And as I reached the small hut, there was reveled beyond it a viewing of what sat beyond the mountain itself: the vague outline of a city became visible in the far distance, and a vast ocean which sat even farther off upon the city's edge. It must have been the sea the man referred to when he spoke of the other teachers leaving, I thought.

The interior of the hut itself was a sparse but graceful one, bearing not within it but the essential effects one needs to live and know some necessary amount of comfort. Yet it felt strangely of a kind of warmth to me, despite having not been occupied for many years.

I returned the swords to their mounts on the wall adjacent the bed, and began to look around. For I could not help but be silently curious as to whom the woman had been that once dwelt there.

A handful of books were scattered around, on the shelf by the bed and the small desk near where the swords were mounted, a few candles and trinkets you'd expect to find: parchment and ink, a jug for bearing water and some cups for drinking. But nothing that gave me insight into whom she might've been, or what could explain the sadness in the man's eyes when he spoke of her.

I began to make my way back down to the training circle, and knew that I would have to ask the man myself.

As I arrived he stood waiting, breathing gently and looking to the distant sky as the morning light became the day.

"Who was she?" I broached gently. "…The woman who lived up there?"

At this his gaze fell from the sky to the ground before him and he drew a deep breath. "Someone who once meant a great deal to me," he said. "Someone who in fact still does. And I'm sure always will. But now is not quite the time for that tale. I will tell you the story when the moment is right," he said turning to me. "For now we will continue training."

I nodded to him silently, respecting his wishes to keep this subject private for the time.

"Next," he began after a brief pause, "we shall practice something simpler and slower—you will tend the gardens with me. Now that you are leaning to focus, and through that focus, cultivate the presence of your mind, you must next foster its stillness.

For as we tend the gardens you will sit within this presence you are learning and come to know the silences of your soul. You will take what time is needed to become aware of your every task and deed, performing each with conscious, careful intent. You will give yourself space enough to hear the wind and smell the soil, to feel the earth and learn the plants. And by that manner of being, come to find yourself, not one thing amongst many, but that *you,* as all things, are rather only a great many things, of *one*."

I followed the man into the gardens of the mountain top, which grew thicker and deeper and ever more encompassing than I could have perceived from beyond them. They were rich and lush, vast and sprawling, nearly intoxicating in the gorgeousness of their density, somewhere I would often wander in many a free moment to become happily lost.

The man led me to a large area of uncultivated space. "This area here shall be yours," he said. "And you will begin with these." At this he produced from his pocket a small leather wrapping containing a variety of seeds. "First you must till and make ready the earth, then once so, you may begin planting. For there is not that can well take root if the soil is not first set."

And so I did. I tilled the soils that first day of our training and began planting.

Over time, the man taught me many things as we worked in the gardens: what various uses and properties the many plants growing there had, the best ways to cultivate and maintain them, how they could be processed and stored, and even what ways they could be applied together in a seemingly endless host of combinations and proportions to create innumerably differing effects. But mostly what I learned was what delicateness and precision was required for any of it to occur at all— time and persistence, trial and error, effort and work.

As we finished the training of the first day, having eaten and rested some earlier, the evening became open to me.

"You may take this time now for whatever you wish, my boy," he said. "Review the lessons of the day, explore the books upon the self, walk the mountain top and breathe the air, whatever you find to be most needed that will suit your soul."

***

The evening air was growing cool as I stepped out onto the mountain top. The sky was veiled in beautiful textured colors strewn across its scattered clouds from the twilight glow, and I began to walk amongst the ruins, reviewing what I had learned since I'd arrived. I knew then what I had to do, I told myself. For it was possible I could change what had become of the lands of my home.

"If I can learn to wield my mind and master my thoughts, I can change my shape," I said aloud as I walked the ruins, "and by that effect taken, shape in turn what is around me. For it is only by the shape so taken we make the world what it is." It seemed a steep task, to be sure. Yet it was equally as possible I knew in that moment, and *possible* was all I needed.

The man was right: I had tasted the essence of something I would require for this fight that night in the valley of the banners and chimes, some resolve, some unshakeable thing. I had found something which would not permit itself to be broken *by*, or subject *to*, any manner of darkness or fear, no matter how strong. Yet it was still fleeting to me then, still untamed and unwieldy, and I knew I would have to capture this place if I was to win the fight and take back the lands of my home. But again I thought to myself as I walked— it was possible, was it not? I had felt it once, could I not find it longer?

I came to the gathering place with its columns and its torches, long unused. I stood upon its furthest point which reached to the edge of the mountain and overlooked the valley and world below; all now veiled in the textured fading light, as the deep satin sky gave birth to night.

"I do not know how to return to you," I spoke to the lands of my home, overlooking all the world that fell before me. "Even if I am able to learn this that must be learned, I still do not know how to return to you."

—But I knew also that it did not yet matter. For even if I could have returned to the lands of my home in that moment, I would not have been ready to do so. And even if I carried forth through this journey, seeking not but the way to be back upon them, I would return to them equally as lost as I felt there, in that place then. For I would return with none of the answers or strengths to confront what must be faced.

"We can never depart from the things that have not yet taught us what we need to know," the poet had said to me once, and I was beginning to understand what this meant.

It did not yet matter that I did not know the way back, I thought. It mattered only that I had found something which would help me once I did. I could change what had become of the lands of my home, I knew in that moment, if I *did*, and *learned*, what so needed to be.

And nothing else was yet important.

***

So I gave myself over then entirely to the work of the days, to the effort and the focus and the discipline of its toil. Which though difficult and tiring at times, was not in vain. For as the weeks began to pass, turning to months by count of the new moons, I found myself growing silently stronger than ever I knew possible.

For I became upon that mount a quiet steward of my mind, a gentle watchman holding silent vigils, to every passing thought and thing which roused, to every stirring feeling and encounter which took subsequent response within me.

I began to wake there many nights within my dreams, for so mindful of the stirring of my thoughts had I become that even sleep could not take my presence from me. But a master of all things within them did I grow to be, conjuror of anything I could imagine, manipulator and wielder of whatsoever was before me.

Many nights within my dreams I found myself back upon the lands of my home, practicing the act of ridding it of what darkness had taken root there, and purging it of any fell things to restore it to life. But more often I found myself off upon some grand adventure beyond that moment, freed of the darkness to go and *do*, and *see*, and *know* as I saw fit. Often entertaining the very characters within my dreams by making objects in the surrounding environment move, or appear and disappear. Or flying around through them, perfectly weightless and controlled, for both the pleasure of mine, and the marvel of theirs.

Most mornings as I woke beyond these dreams, I did so before my eyes had even opened, becoming conscious of the feeling of the room, and the scents of the air, what sounds stirred about me, before I would rise to meet the man, and begin a new day of training.

And as I grew to achieve this oneness within myself, I began to understand how I was affecting the nature of my own shape.

"It is all and only a matter of consciousness, my boy," the man said to me one day, "all and only about being made aware, not only to the outward occurrences external to you, but to the very shape what thoughts manifest within, become. For they are making you, and you them, and *you* the world, and the world then reflecting back and becoming you once more, casting its shape taken again in your direction. A seemingly endless, infinite loop, shifting its course and changing its shape, with you in the midst of it.

Your task, though great in its totality, is not really any different in principle than anything else. You told me once how on your journey here you learned to take the shape of a jester, and in that shape you were assisted on your way. To confront the gravity of what you faced, you became levity, to counter the depths of its severity, you became the weightlessness of laughter. What I now wish you to understand is not really so different than that. For to defeat the darkness you need only learn to become the light. To counter what fear the darkness brings, bravery unbroken, and to soar beyond the pitfalls of its uncertainty, faith that is capable of going forth consciously into the unknown.

—Light, breath, and being," he said. "Light, breath, and being, my boy. *Become it*. Become that which permeates through all, and you will all-become."

I did not know at the time if I understood his words or not, but I listened and I tried. I ventured, and slowly I became.

For nearly five years to the day I stayed with the man upon the mountain, living with and learning from him, growing and becoming in what ways I needed. I stayed until I had dove down deep, to the very furthest reaches of my self and soul, until I had mastered my mind and what strengths in me would need be to change the lands of my home. I stayed until there was not a thought within me to which I was unaware, and not an aspect of my consciousness which did not feel itself in kinship to all other things.

I stayed until the day I needed stay no more, and I heard the very infinite breath which guides all that be.

For one morning as I ascended the steps to the dwelling on the highest point of the mountain top, returning the swords to their proper place as I had done so many times before, something occurred that never before had: I saw a woman as I approached entering the dwelling before me, clothed in black with darkest hair and fairest skin, turning before entering and looking back, as though beckoning silently onward those who followed behind her.

I entered and found her having laid upon the bed by the windows open, breathing gently and closing her eyes, listening with all her being to all that was.

And though I knew it to be only a fragment of things past as I looked on, a ghost or relic of times former, it could not have been more real to me.

I rested the swords upon the desk adjacent the bed and approached, laying precisely where the woman had in this vision which played out before me. I folded my arms as she had first, and then laid them by my side. I drew deep the breaths of the air about me and shut my eyes.

And through the open windows of that simple abode, there rode in the aromas of the garden on the cool air— I slipped slumberously into that floral scent, the warmth upon my skin, and what daylight drifted in. It was peace in all my senses that wrapped me in a kind of thoughtless comfort, to which I happily resigned my consciousness; I strayed away, forfeiting what claim I may or may not have had to any woe, abandoning my thoughts to the gentle burgeoning of my spirit's gentle roam. And there in that place was I lost, but there strangely was I home, saved inside a sunray, of those earthen scents was I then clothed. And I could hear there what the man had spoken often of so much. I could hear the way that wove itself amongst the universe and all that be, that infinite breath which became all things. I could hear it as it beckoned and as it sung, quiet and soft, gentle and strange, as it stirred amongst the air and the sun.

For what felt to be many a hundred year I drifted in this place, drawing deep into me whatever it was, that I might not lose it, or *myself*, be lost without it. And slowly as I did eventually return to my own being, I opened my eyes and found my body to be laying precisely where it had, and only a matter of hours had in fact passed.

***

I descended from the height of this dwelling upon the mountain top and found the man standing in wait, as the sun of the same day had begun to set, and the fire he had struck amongst the columns of the old gathering place burned bright.

"You found something up there..." he said softly as I neared, "...something you hadn't in your time here before."

I stood only in silence before him for a moment, knowing not what words could possibly have been spoken to convey it.

"Take a seat, my friend," he said. And so I did, nestling into the soft glow of the flames, and the shine of the heavens above.

"You have heard it now," he continued, "the way which binds all things, the very breath giving birth to all that be. And as you can now hear it, you shall never again be without it. For it is not some dream you shall faint recall upon waking you now know, but the very substance that is dreaming any of it at all."

"You never told me the story of who she was," I said, speaking of the woman in black. And the fire glistened in the eyes of the man as he gazed deep into it.

"It is not so uncommon a tale to be told, my friend," he said to me slowly, "but rather more uncommon to be known. For we met upon the road so very long ago first venturing here, as we had both come seeking the same thing. By the valley of the banners and chimes we encountered one another, seeing at once in the other's eyes the same dream of what was sought. We spoke little..." he said pausing, "that first meeting we had. For such were words smaller than what was then said in silent looks alone. I *knew* her the moment that I saw her. As she *knew* me. Like an old friend long absent, or a soul separate, really of one. Together we made the ascent of the mountain, and together we were tested by the pass; together we uncovered the stairs, and eventually grew to dwell and teach here."

"You shared that space up there, didn't you?" I asked the man, and he nodded silently.

"We were the first," he said. "The first of the teachers, and the first who dwelt here. And for many years occupied that space together...but all things must come to an end."

"What happened?" I asked, "Did she leave with the others?"

"She did," he said. "We loved each other, more than we had ever loved anyone, that is not untrue. But as our own paths had once brought us together in this life, so too did they eventually move us apart."

"But why?" I asked.

"Just as it was my time to stay, it was hers to go. As I had not yet done all that I had come here to do, she felt she had fulfilled her purpose in this place. It did not seem so simple or easy a thing at the time, but that is the truth of it. We could not either of us justify doing what was best for the one, if it was not what was best for the other. So we did what so few seem to and chose to do what was best for both, even if it meant we were no longer together. For you do not truly love a thing, if in the keeping of your own love for it, cannot permit it to be completely what it is."

"Why could I see her up there before?" I asked him.

"Call it an echo of something she left behind," he said.

"I don't understand," I said to him.

"I'm not sure that I understand it myself," he returned, "but I have *known* it. We scatter fragments of ourselves in the places that we have been and the things we have encountered, in what we have done, there are traces of us left behind. And here it seems some fragment of her spirit has helped teach you what she helped teach me so long ago. For as I told you when you first arrived, she was the wisest and most graceful person I have ever known. And though my heart has broken in ways at our parting, happier am I to have ever known her at all… There is nothing more I need now here teach you," he said.

The man and I both fell silent and looked to the stars. For they were growing and blossoming above us in the satin sky, and it struck me strange that even here, in this most learned and wise of places, there could be things not quite yet understood— what ways the courses of love between beings will take, and the lasting effects of our deeds. But so it was. The man had learned much in his days, but still were there mysteries of things to be uncovered by him.

And there amongst that mystery unknown, and the breath of all that be, I found a kind of peace which stretched, not only to the furthest reaches of me, but out into and through the space of all time and things, ever conceived.

***

As the morning light broke I awoke in my bed upon the twelfth mountain for the final time. I gathered up my things and had tea with the man for what would be the last. We savored the familiarity of it, having both grown accustomed, and knowing what was next to come.

When the moment had arrived and there was no more left to be said, the man and I gathered on the far side of the mountain top and spoke our final farewells.

"Where forth from here will you go?" he asked, as the space of all the land beyond the mountain sat soaked in the midmorning sun.

"What other way can so be gone?" I returned to him. "—Forward, *on,* to wherever the way beckons next. For there is no way around, but *through*."

At this the man smiled softly the quiet satisfaction of having taught a student well. "This now belongs to you then," he said, presenting me the sword which I had trained in my years with him. Graciously, and knowing the gravity of what this meant to him, I accepted silently, inclining my head before fastening the blade to my hip.

"Thank you." I said to him. "Thank you my friend. If there's anything I can do to repay you for what you've done—"

"—you owe me nothing, dear Galloway," he interrupted. "*You owe me nothing.* Trust in what you have learned and follow the signs as they beckon, they will not lead you astray."

"What will become of *you?*" I asked him in return.

"I shall remain some while longer I think," he said, as though first truly considering it. "I have a feeling there are others who will soon come seeking. Perhaps there are some amongst them who will wish remain and begin teaching themselves. There is a new age I think, beginning."

"Farewell my friend," I said with a heavy breath, inclining my head to the man in silent admiration. "I wish you nothing but the best."

"Let me know, Galloway," he said as I moved to depart, "let me know what becomes. For the shadows which now occupy your lands will not so easily relinquish what they have claimed. They will strike to the very deepest reaches of you when you return. But if you are able to do what you need and must, only ever will this place be a breath away. Come back and tell me what becomes."

"I will," I said to him. "You can be sure of that."

And so with both a fondness and a sorrow in my heart, I turned away from the man upon the mountain and began making my way down its other side, to the city and the sea which lay beyond.

***

Part IV: The Storm

I knew not what the way before me had next in store. The spires and towers of the city rose up against the horizon ahead, and it was clear I would reach its gates sometime the following day.

It had been nearly eight years since I first found myself on the shore with the fellows, and this felt both to be far too short a time, and yet equally, too long— too long to have been absent and severed from my home, yet too short to have contained all that my days had since leaving.

Though I knew with peace in my heart as I walked that I could not change the past as it had been, nor the incidents which set me on this path, I could not help but begin to feel a measure of weariness grow within me for the length of my journey. It seemed unfair, or strange, or perhaps cruel even, that such time and effort should be required to restore a thing which ought never be lost to begin with. And yet so it was. The journey could not be ended before it was done. I would have to carry on.

It was possible, I thought to myself again —as I had after that first day training with the man— it was possible I could change what had become of the lands of my home. And I needed to remind myself of this. For once I had believed that they were gone forever, and that there was nothing which could be done. And now not only had it become *possible* to change them, I *knew* that I possessed the ability to do so. For I had become upon that mount something which I never thought myself capable of: a silent master of my own thoughts and self. I had grown to know the world and all that be, the infinite breath dreaming this life into being now swam irrefutably within me. I had felt the light of this world as though it was my very own presence, and I could not so swiftly dismiss these things, despite what time it had yet taken.

***

As I crossed beyond the threshold of the city in the afternoon of the following day, it sprawled out, fantastic and strange to me. For never had I see so many inhabitants of a single place, and certainly not in quite some time.

Everywhere I turned there was a sight to behold and something being done: merchants and shopkeepers selling their wares; busy travelers heading from one place to another; a hundred scents of many dozen things being cooked and stewed, steeped and baked, filled the air. The sounds of its chatter, the clattering of its steps met my ears, resonating as both ruckus and melody to me then.

I carried forth through its streets and its spaces, feeling myself to be both everywhere and nowhere amongst them. For everywhere was there something to be done, and yet nothing within me there to do. Everywhere I turned was a place for the making of a life or the becoming of a trade, and yet I could not tarry amongst them.

For my heart could perceive that not in any of them was there to be found what I sought: the way back home, and the reconciling of what was there. Not amongst the smiths or the potters, the chandlers or the apothecaries, was I to then find what was needed.

I climbed the highest hill of the city and took rest upon a bench overlooking the sea beyond and knew not where next to go. I took the stone from my pocket and the feather of the raven that had come to me on the twelfth mountain from my satchel, holding each in one hand.

What had the man meant when he said that this stone was more than just a totem? I wondered. For it still seemed to me only a token of my home, despite him having told me that it was something other.

I held the stone flat in the palm of my hand and closed my eyes, making silent the space within my mind and began to listen for the way that would next beckon me on: there were the sounds of the city about me and the steps of its inhabitants, the murmur of voices near and far, and the crashing of the sea in the distance on the salty air. The cries of the gulls above played gently in my ears, and tiny wafts of mist began to shower softly on my skin.

—The gulls and the sea, the salt in the air, and the crashing waves grew louder and stronger and nearer, *becoming* the very space I had made silent within. And the wind that carried the mist began to stir more surely, circling round until it had grown strong enough to whip the stone from my hand and it began tumbling down the street before me.

I picked up and followed swiftly, keeping pace so as not to lose sight of it. Down the street it went, tumbling and bouncing and seeming to follow a course entirely of its own. When at last it came to rest, we had reached the docks at the edge of the city, and a mighty vessel that was harbored there.

Her three masts rose up steeply and proud before me, and she seemed to be of the finest making; a vessel forged with the greatest of care and workmanship, fit for any undertaking or passage. The men of her crew were busily loading crates of provisions from the docks to where they were stored beneath her decks, and her captain stood by watching.

As I gazed upon this sight, the captain and his ship in view, the waters in which the vessel sat stretched far out to the horizon where the sun had begun to set, and the sea which calls all things unto her began to beckon me on in her vastness. And I could not help but to heed the call.

For my heart could perceive as I looked upon them that nomads of the seas were they, the captain and his crew, wanderers and traders and riders of the tides, having no true port of harbor but the open water itself, and the very winds which swept them on.

Leaning down I collected the stone and put it back in my pocket. Approaching slowly I spoke to the captain. "When do you depart?" I asked him.

"Upon the morrow," he replied. "When the men have rested and the winds resume."

"Where do you sail to next?"

"To wherever the winds do bellow," he said with an undercurrent of excitement looming in his voice for this uncertainty.

"And have you room for another?" I finished.

"What do you know of sailing, dear boy?" he questioned me in return.

"Nothing that I cannot learn," I said.

"And what do you know of *the sea*?" he pressed.

"Only that she calls me unto her," I answered honestly.

The captain paused for a moment as though considering this and smiled slightly. With a fire looming in his eyes he nodded swiftly. "Well that is enough," he said, accepting my request to sail with him. "True, you can be taught the vessel, but I cannot teach you the spirit that will set foot upon her decks."

"Permission then to come aboard, captain?" I asked in formality.

"Granted!" he returned to me, pleased with the exchange. "Young master—?"

"Galloway," I said.

"Young master Galloway then. *Make way!*" And flagged me on to join the ranks.

I assisted the men in loading the final crates of provisions onto the ship, and then stayed aboard for the evening as the rest of the crew ventured out into the city for what time they would have there. I wanted to acquaint myself with the vessel's decks and holds, her ropes and her riggings and facets.

It seemed perhaps a strange becoming to me at the time, to take up passage on a vessel bound for no-where in particular. But no stranger in truth, I thought, than anything else which had been my journey till then. For it was the only way forth that did not seem itself to be an obvious wrong, and I knew in my heart that I could not stay amongst the city, or that even if I did, there was nothing there which would carry me on.

I had learned enough by then to trust that the way forth was not always one which was apparent, or contained at its beginning, a clear and certain end. For my days had taught me that even that which seems in-viable and destined to last forever, may in fact change, that there was nothing truly certain about certainty, so therefore nothing really to be feared amongst the un-known.

***

The captain alone stayed too aboard that first evening, walking the planks of the deck and staring off to the final rays of light left shimmering upon the water's surface from the setting sun. He seemed to be quietly contemplating something.

"That is a fine blade you carry," he said, as I came to stand next to him at the rail, observing the sun as it descended far across the sea. "Can you use it?" he asked.

I turned and met his gaze, which was locked fiercely on mine, equal parts challenge and play in his eyes, and nodded to him silently.

"Show me," he said, drawing the sword at his hip and making a few paces of distance between us.

I turned and drew my own, the metal shimmering audibly as it was freed from the sheath, and assumed a combative stance. It occurred to me that I had never before sparred with anyone but the man and was eager to see what would happen.

The captain launched into a small volley of attacks, each of which I parried successfully but uncertainly before returning a few of my own. His style was somewhat more eccentric than I was accustomed to, less composed and direct, more wild and full of flourish. It seemed perhaps fitting, I thought, given the roving nature of his lifestyle, that I could not quite be sure where his attacks were moving to. "You have good form," he said after the first exchange. "Someone taught you well."

The captain carried into another bout of attacks and counters. "Tell me truly," he continued amongst the clash and shimmer of the exchange. "Why do you really seek passage aboard my ship?"

The question troubled me at first, and I parried and countered his attacks with increasing voracity. I knew that I couldn't explain to him in full the happenings that had been my days to lead me to that moment. But nor could I entirely dismiss his inquiry. Even if he was capable of understanding my tale unto that point, I hadn't the words at that time to yet tell it. I had confided in the man when I first arrived upon the mount, but my journey had been younger then, and he, a different breed of person I knew capable of understanding it. Too many more things had yet transpired in my days to explain simply why I needed passage then and there, or how I found myself to be in that place.

I decided to respond with a fragment of the truth, "I am seeking something I do not yet know how to find," I said to him. "Something of mine that was lost."

"Lost at sea?" he returned to me.

"In a fashion," I replied, thinking back to my arrival in this place. "Something dear to me, something that makes my days the lesser if not found."

"Then perhaps we are seekers of similar things," he said amidst the clash of the blades that continued.

"I thought you went wherever the winds took you," I replied.

"We do," he said in return, "but that does not mean we are not looking for something amongst them."

"What then are you seeking?" I asked him.

"A land that has never before been reached by any," he said. "Somewhere no soul has ever set foot."

At once I thought of what the man had told me when he said that something different was happening in my days than had seemed to occur before, as none had yet been afflicted with such a thing and returned to tell the tale of it. Indeed— I *was* seeking a place that had never been reached, I thought. Or at the very least, somewhere that *I* had never been.

The captain and I finished a final series of attacks and counters, neither having bested or faulted to the other and paused. "Come with me for a moment," he said, as he sheathed his sword. I obliged and sheathed my own, following him across the deck and into his quarters at the stern of the ship.

We entered into a gorgeous wooden hold, dimly illuminated by the candles which sat burning within it, and the lantern upon the captain's desk. The room was filled with a number of maps, charts, and navigation tools scattered about it; various trinkets and tokens dangled from whatever they could be hung upon, and numerous volumes of old books sat stowed wherever they would not shift or slide about in times at sea.

"Why do you have all this and not use it?" I asked the captain, referring to the maps and navigation tools he possessed.

"As I said," he returned to me, "there is a place that I am seeking, but it is not one which can yet be found or sought by any such means. I have spent my life until recently, sailing the seas as a merchant trader and offering passage to those with coin enough to pay for it, heading from here to there, one place to another, always upon a course that was charted, and always upon one that was not my own. But my heart does not yearn for these things. It longs to find a land where none have yet gone. It longs to forge forth into waters which harbor no bearing or beacon. It longs to confront the unknown. I am not a man of the path that has been laid, *but of the laying—* that is this man's breath full made. It seems you have arrived at a most fortuitous time, young master Galloway," he said turning to me, "if the seeking of what you do not know how to find is what brought you here. For this voyage tomorrow shall be our maiden into waters truly unknown."

"Have you not already begun?" I asked him.

"We no longer sail under the command of another, that is true, and not for some time. But this past year has been one of preparation, gathering our crew and amassing a hold of coin and provisions for the waters ahead."

"And what will you do if your stores are depleted?" I asked him curiously.

"Much the same as we have always done," he replied, "ferry precious cargo for a time and those who require transport. But we shall do so upon terms of our own if needed. And make no mistake," he said with a gleam in his eye, "many a sunken wreck are there amongst these seas for the scavenging."

I could not help the small grin which crossed my face at the captain. For the spirit of his present days and mood was undeniably infectious.

"Join me for a cup of wine, young master Galloway," he spoke next. "And tell me more of this that you do not yet know how to find. Perhaps we can assist one another."

I reached within my satchel and removed from it the goblet the chief fellow had gifted to me, wiping gently away the dust and grime which had amassed in its un-use. Seating myself in the chair opposite the captain's desk, he uncorked a bottle of the finest vintage I had ever tasted and pored.

"So then," he continued, "tell me what it was that brought you here."

***

For many hours that night the captain and I spoke, trading words and tales of our times, finding within the other an unexpected and sudden confidant, a new friend curiously aligned at the time of our meeting for where we were each needing to go. He, a land never before reached by any. And myself, the passage home.

As our conversation slowly made way to its natural end, the captain rose from the desk and showed me down to the crew's quarters on one of the lower decks where a hammock awaited me. It was slung between two posts and nestled amongst some of the crates we had loaded earlier. "Settle in and make yourself comfortable Galloway, this here shall be home for a time."

"Good evening captain," I said, and settled in easily for the night.

***

The following morning the bell which hung at the helm was sounded by the captain, calling all crew to gather on deck for the initial embarkment.

I fell into ranks that morning at the lowest— ready to swab the decks and tidy the cabins and would begin working my way up. Despite what bond the captain and I had formed the previous evening, he would not permit me ascend the ranks faster than I was due or deserved. A fact for which I respected him immensely. For nothing was there withheld on his vessel from those who had earned it, but nor was there anything given in privilege alone.

As we assembled that morning he spoke, "Greetings fair gentlemen and thanks, for your company alone but also your spirit. It is into what waters await we go; to whatever uncertain harbors that beckon, and whatever unknown shores, loom. If there are any among you who have had other thoughts and no longer wish any part of this venture, you may leave now, to no admonishment of your character, or dismal of your choice."

Each man looked round and yet none moved from where their feet were planted aboard the deck.

"The destination is well and good," the captain continued, "—wherever it is that may be wished these wind to carry us *to*. But let us not forget that the spirit of the journey itself is upon what very waters will ferry us from one land to another, and not in the land itself."

And looking round then the captain paused, taking in the crew of men he had assembled, and what unbroken vigilance existed amongst us. The winds of the beckoning sea began to stir and sway, playing at the masts and prodding at the hull, rocking and moving us as they did.

"Well then," he said, "what more to be spoken? The winds are ready! *Make way!*" And the men sprung to action, drawing the anchor and hoisting the sails, readying the vessel for her voyage into whatever waters did so await.

***

I stood that morning upon the bow, watching as our sails caught the wind and began to push us out into the open sea. For my duty then was a small one, and I had little to do on this first embarkment but look on in curious wonder.

Swiftly and steadily were we pushed out from where we had been docked, and slowly did the city line upon the horizon fade to imperceivable faintness behind us. And then suddenly, in a moment it seemed, *we were there*— out into the open, unknown, everything. The aimless sea everlasting reaching out, harboring somewhere upon its vast horizon the potential for anything under creation to manifest itself and become. We were at once everywhere and nowhere then, adrift in a great vacant divide, between wherever had been, and anywhere there was to be gone.

"Secure the line, young master Galloway!" one of the men shouted to me, inviting me over and snapping me back to the moment. I obliged, tying the rope with a knot he instructed to me then.

"Fastly tied!" he piped. "And *well*!" giving the line a swift tug. "You might make a fine sailor yet!" and slapped me on the back.

Quickly did the men of the captain's crew take me under their wing that first voyage, teaching me what knowledge they could of sailing and the sea; what ropes and riggings there were to the ship, and some of the tricks they had learned in their days.

The winds which swept us first beyond the city carried us some few weeks out, to a small line of archipelagos where the skies grew sullen and the waters, frigid. The chill which hung in the air bit at the lips and lungs of those who breathed it, and it reminded me of some of the mountain tops I had encountered when searching for the man.

As we approached one of the islands of the chain, we spied a small dock stretching out from it and a few tiny vessels anchored off its coast.

The houses and structures visible beyond the shore were small and unassuming, distributed somewhat sporadically upon the island's relatively barren hillsides.

It was obvious at once that this chain was neither unfound land, nor likely for myself the passage home, but the captain was undeterred.

"Well," he said, tossing his hands up in the air and beginning to lower the plank onto the dock that we might disembark, "what point would there be to arrive and go not the looking?! To venture, but not *see*? *Embark*, yet port not the harbor of one's finding?— sounds of a life only part lived to me," and then set first feet down the plank and onto the dock. The rest of us soon followed behind, exchanging silent glances with one another that we hadn't a better reason not to go.

The villagers seemed hardly to fetch a look at our arrival, not likely because this was a bustling port, but more because they seemed content in its isolation and wanted not to be bothered.

We therefore proceeded gently into their midst, seeking not to disturb, only explore. Slowly we wandered through the rural, simple streets, exchanging silent nods of pleasantries to those who looked up as we went past. Though mostly they seemed issued only to confirm that we meant no harm, and then the villagers would return to what they had been doing before.

I did as some part of my soul was still much accustomed to at that time and struck off without the crew to ascend the highest of the foothills which resided on the island, a small ways off beyond the village.

As I reached the peak of it there arrived at my feet the large feather of an eagle upon the wind. I collected it and stowed it in my satchel, taking it as a favorable sign that I was on the right path.

From the height of this foothill I could perceive another ship arriving off in the distance, and that as the villagers glimpsed its coming, some of them began to gather near to the docks.

I quickly descended the foothill, rejoining the captain and the rest of the crew, who also stood nearby watching what was unfolding.

From the streets of the village an elderly woman was being lead to the ship, assisted by those who appeared to be her family, or perhaps only those who cared for her.

"What's happening?" I asked the captain quietly.

"She is heading for the journey that is next," he said almost imperceivably softly to me, and with a high degree of reverence and respect, "to what realm awaits beyond this life."

It was one of the vessels the man had told me about when he spoke of the other teachers leaving, I realized.

Slowly the woman was helped down the street and onto the ship where she stood upon the stern and gave a gentle wave back. A measure of peace was spread across her face as though some part of her spirit had already gone, and only now was her body to make the final stage of the journey.

As the vessel set sail and disappeared from view, the villagers who had gathered dispersed, and only did there remain upon the docks those who had helped her to the ship. They stood for some long time into the night, keeping this vigil of their grief.

We stayed that evening a far ways down upon the shore, wanting not to intrude upon their vigil with our departure. A somberness overtook the group as we sat about the fire that night, speaking to each other much of life and death.

"It should not be so hard a thought to confront," began one of the men, "that one day— *one day it will be the last*. Never to rise again nor draw another breath. It is so strange to me now that *all* of it should pass. That not these lips with which I have kissed, nor these arms with which I have loved, shall remain. Not what fists I have raised in anger, nor what feet have carried me in excitement or toil —the same— but all, *all shall cease remain.*"

"What would allow you then to pass with peace?" I asked of him.

"I suppose only to know that while I had it, I held it," he said. "That as I was alive, *I lived.* That I had *been,* in my *being* at all. To know this as I know now that I draw what very breaths shall one day pass. To know that I had met days filled of both quiet stirrings and desperate seekings, of both piercing marvels and a moment's more passing pleasures. And that I had not failed to rise," he added, "to the greatest of my yearnings and potential... to know that I hadn't missed it," he finished, "whatever this life is at all."

The group of us all sat silent about the fire, thinking on his words and drawing in those more simple of things: the crackle of sound and the flicker of light, the twinge of salt which hung in the fresh sea air and the mood of the night that began to envelop us.

"To greet each day as though it were the very last," said the captain.

"—Or yet, *the very first,*" added the crewman who had spoken with a playful grin.

"To greet each day then with the knowledge that one is alive and at it again?" amended the captain.

"Aye good captain, *that we are alive and at it again.*"

For a time we fell silent and looked from the fire to the stars, from the stars to the sea and back again. We seemed then all to be meditating upon the same thing, though spoke not of it to each other aloud: that we were then amongst the breath of such a living as had been described. For we were upon the very seas of our seeking, broken off and out into a great and new wide-open. We were at the mercy of what winds stirred to take us where they would, prepared to encounter all we did from here till there. And there was a comfort to be drawn in this, knowing that we had moved in the direction of our lives, and of our *living,* even if we did not know what would follow next, even if the seas were uncharted, and the course itself, unknown. We were where we needed to be then, as close as could be gotten to where we sought to go, without actually knowing the way.

"Upon the morrow again then gents?" said the captain, seeming to address our collective thoughts, that we would *rise* and *be at it again.*

If we had not so before this moment, the group of us then found ourselves undoubtedly to be upon the same voyage with one another.

And slowly amongst these thoughts, the fire, and the sounds and scents of the sea did we slip into the depths of sleep, before rising to set sail again.

***

When the morning light broke I caught up with the captain at the docks, needing to speak with him about a thought I had found as I slept.

"Captain," I said, "I was wondering— would you mind if I put to use some of those instruments you have in your cabin?"

He said nothing at first but shot me a look of inquiry as we walked. "I was thinking," I continued, "even if we don't know where we're *going*, it might prove helpful to have a log of where we've *been:* to chart what course the winds have taken us on and anything we find your maps might not already contain. It's possible there are things we could learn from knowing where we've gone, and what we've encountered along the way."

He raised his eyebrow to me in a way that indicated he seemed fond of the idea. "I would've let them gather dust," he said. "But it is a fine thought. What do you aim we stand to learn?"

"Truthfully I am not yet sure," I replied. "But the thought came to me as I slept and I can't seem to dismiss it. Perhaps it was the woman we saw last night or the exchange which followed. I don't know. I have only the feeling that what we'll encounter amongst these seas are things we are meant to. And for that then, whatever knowledge may be gleaned from them shall be better served if we have charts and records to look back upon."

The captain nodded. "You shall have access to my instruments whenever you require. And I can teach you what you'll need to learn for navigation and cartography. Sounds as though you anticipate us spending some time upon these seas. Do you think we are long out?" he asked as we made way up the plank and set foot on deck.

I thought about it for a moment as we ascended the stairs and came to stand by the helm. I recalled suddenly what the poet had said to me long ago and gave his words then to the captain, "If something is worth it to be learned or done— what matter is the time?"

***

Over the following months I grew to know the compass and the sextant, spending the evenings charting our course with the captain, and the days growing more proficient as a sailor on his ship.

From the north to the west we went, from the west to the south, and then back north again before heading east. We were at the welcomed mercy of the winds then, being lead by them wherever they took us to go.

To a small island of apothecaries and healers they swept us soon after departing from the island with the village, and we encountered a temple many centuries active there, long sought for its restorative medicines. The monks who occupied and tended it saw to the treatment of the crew, several of whom possessed limps or other minor ailments, and upon hearing of what experience I had, gifted to me a variety of plants from their gardens with which I could brew tinctures and tonics to keep us well as we sailed.

The monks declined payment of any kind for their services, yet the captain, ever respectful but disobedient, left a small pouch of coins stashed behind a vase on the temple steps as we exited.

As we made way from port upon our departure, I could see a young boy find them, and in his excitement to show his friends, held the pouch high above his head and began running down the steps, scattering the coins everywhere as he went. Even from the ship the cling-clang of coins could be faintly heard, and the captain and I chuckled as we watched the boy and his friends hurry to gather them up.

***

In the days and weeks which followed our arrival at the temple island, I began using a space amongst the crew's quarters for the keeping and cultivating of the plants given to me. For it had good light and was adjacent to the hammock in which I slept. It fastly became a common occurrence for the crew to seek me out in their time of need or ailment, and I would make best use of what skills the man had taught me to distill or brew something which would aid them.

As the months grew on, we began to find ourselves operating in only a greater rhythm with one another, and with what path the winds cut upon the very seas themselves, never growing much tired of it.

For it felt to us somehow as though we would set sail again each new time we woke, rising and making our way to the top deck, casting our ready eyes once more to the horizon, wondering what new unknowns would next await upon it. For whether rising by day to man the riggings, or night to keep watch as we went, there was not ever a feeling born amongst us that the seas had become stale, or tired, or vacant. Always did there seem to be promise possible amongst them. For we were aimless then but not un-wanting, *wanting*, but not to the ruin of our selves nor to the loss of what journey we were on. We were vibrant in our readiness and our eagerness to uncover what there was to be next found, and fates willing, what we sought amongst those winds and waters unknown, but grew not hopelessly dependent upon it, nor crazed by loss or defeat when the objects of our seeking did not appear as we wished them to. We became voyagers of our own fates upon those seas, vigilant and adrift, both steadfast and sturdy, having pledged our spirits equally to the uncertain and the sought, to both the aimless sea, and the diligently sailed.

Every port or reef or gulf that appeared before us we would spy keenly, investigating it to its end, whatever that might've been, and to wherever it might've lead.

And though at times there were promising lands we would spot, brave new territories appearing at their first immanence in our telescopes, leading us to hope and dream and wonder keenly that they were the visages after which we yearned, ultimately proving not, still— we sailed on.

For time and time again, no matter where the winds took us, there seemed to have been something we gained from them; whether knowledges needed or provisions required; times which tested our mettle as sailors and men, or the occasional reef or cove not more than once unknown beauties to us which we could then behold— all seemed to ultimately impart something of value we previously lacked.

In the fourth year of our time upon the seas, the captain and crew promoted me to their quartermaster. For I had been assuming multiple duties for some time by then and had grown exceedingly proficient in nearly all areas of our life at sea, from the ropes and the riggings, to the care of the crew, to the tracking of our course and keeping log of the journey.

I moved into the quartermaster's cabin adjacent the captain's and set up to my liking, bringing with me the plants and vines from the holds bellow which quickly flourished in their new environment, having slowly approached maturation in the years prior and needing more space to grow. I began hosting meetings at the round table there with the captain and members of the crew when off duty, speculating as to what the nature of our path was, or why the winds would take us where they did in times where what we gained from them were not as clear. We would discuss our lives as they shifted and grew, intertwined and changed with one another upon the seas. And quite often we would take time to talk of nothing of importance, drinking what wine we had bartered or traded, or sipping graciously from the captain's reserve.

As the months grew on and became our final three years, they proceeded much in this cycle of sailing and seeking, logging and tracking, conversing and commiserating. We began to notice that what path the winds swept us on was nearly one of a circle which seemed to be closing, imperfect and full of breaks, criss crossing of paths previously sailed, but ultimately of some greater arc narrowing and narrowing. The last year of our time took us on nearly an identical loop of the year which came before it. And as we grew to notice these things, at first only fleeting suspicions, then confirmed by the procession of time, we began to wonder amongst ourselves what the purpose had been, or what we would next do. For it became clear there was nowhere else left to sail.

When the day came that we had at last reached the center of whatever this loop the winds had took us on was— they ceased, our sails fell empty and not a breeze stirred, and we became stalled there. Racing at once to my cabin I plotted the final part of our journey and found indeed that we had come to the exact center of this seven year circle. Taking the map to the helm I showed the captain that our suspicions of the last few years had indeed been correct, and the crew gathered nearby to listen in. A small silence fell between the captain and I, and not so much as a breath could be heard from amongst the crew. After a moment of this, the captain spoke.

"What is it then you think, master Galloway? If the winds which sweep and bellow do not direct our course as we see fit? Where then would you have us venture if there is not a 'where' amongst these seas to which we have not already been? For though the winds have not lead us astray, nor have they brought us to our seeking, either."

"I will not say to you that the winds are bad my friend, for they have lead us here. And *here* is not so fowl or disfavor-able a place. For even discounting all they have given us, at the very least the winds have shown us where *not* amongst these seas the nature of our seeking is. From near and far, and to many wondrous things between we've seen and been, and found exactly where what we're looking for *isn't*— and perhaps it is simply that amongst them we are missing."

"The words are yours," he said in return, inciting me to carry on.

"Well," I continued, "they have taken us everywhere, have they not?" I said pointing to our course upon the map. "For seven years now we have been upon tides and seas uncertain, crossing every manner of what reaches fell before us, venturing far and wide, to expanses here and there and all that came between. We have been made stronger, more capable and more cleaver than we were when we began. We have been enriched by the very experiences we have known. But ever in these years has there been one place the winds themselves have not steered us to. Ever has there been one, exact place. A place we have criss-crossed and passed, circled round, narrowing and narrowing but never once been *to*," I said, pointing at a small, deeply grey spot which loomed in the distance on the horizon.

"It is a storm," said the captain. "Why would we steer ourselves there?"

"…For what lay *beyond* it." I said curiously in return.

"But we have passed that storm before," he said. "There's nothing beyond it we have not already found."

"Yes indeed, we have been *around* it many times," I returned. "By the books I have logged, it seems twelve. And yet we have never once, in all that time, been *through* it. How then can we say with certainty what in fact lay *beyond* it?"

"What then would you have us do, master Galloway?" he asked, a fire beginning to spark in his eyes.

"—Let us see what's on the other side," I replied. "For it seems that the seven year winds have circled our path only nearer and nearer to. And there are some things in this life for which there is no way around my friend, *only through*."

The captain grinned an almost maniacal smile as though something in him might've been awaiting this prompt for a great long time, and seemed then to quietly laugh to himself.

"What is it?" I asked.

"Something I read a long time ago," he said. "Something I think I finally understand."

"What was it?" I asked him.

"Invictus," he said turning to me. "'—I am the master of my fate: I am the captain of my soul.' —Let us face all there is to be faced then, master Galloway. Let us confront all there is to be confronted. Let us put to use every manner of skill and breath of faith, every pulse of courage and surge of daring the winds have swept us to till now, and if at that end there is still not what we seek to be found, then at least we may go forth in peace without it, knowing we could have done no better."

Silently then, and without breaking his eyes from mine, the captain stepped aside and gestured simply with both hands to the helm— granting me, in that moment, command of the ship.

I slung my satchel upon the post near and grasped the helm, calling out the commands to the men who had already sprung to action, having watched the exchange and knowing what next to do.

Our sails billowed audibly as they grew taught and caught the wind of a mighty gale growing behind us.

"Blank blank! Blank blank!" the men called out, whose words were muffled amidst the rage of the winds which growled. At once they began tightening the lines and securing the holds, for already were we cresting upon the first of treacherous waters, and the bow of the ship began arcing its course to point directly into the storm. In an instant it seemed we were upon it, as though the storm itself began advancing *to us*, as much as we were *to it*. Far about and overhead its presence rose round: crashes of lightning struck and flashed as hot, piercing veins across the sky, and mighty claps of thunder echoed out ominous in the rumbling beyond. The veil of clouds into which we were steered loomed from deepest rain soaked grey, to resonant crimson amidst the lighting and setting sun beyond.

Swifter and swifter the gale which carried us grew, moving us as quick as could be gone— into the rains and winds which began to pelt, firing in ferocious torrents of sharp, stinging pain; into the crests of the sea which began to rise as though mountains unto themselves; into the darkness of the clouds which began to obscure and dissolve the day's fleetingly remaining light.

At once I began to doubt the choice I had made, and the trust the captain and the crew had placed in me. For if the waves breaking above the bow did not threaten overflow and sink us, then surely the rains from above did.

Only some dozen minutes into the storm were we and the topsail had torn clean off, splitting a piece of the mast off with it as it went, threatening to strand us where we were if matters became worse.

"Push on boys!" shouted the captain with a raucous laugh that fringed on madness. *"We're not through yet!"*

It was perhaps only some matter of hours we forged the storm, and yet it felt to us to have been a small lifetime; filled in and of itself with every manner of peril and uncertain drama; with actions rising and falling like the very waters themselves: for how many times the ropes became ripped from the hands of the crew, whipping and thrashing about wildly, nearly impossible to be seen or recovered amongst the flashing of the lightning; or how even once regained by the hand, footing upon the incomparably slick deck would be lost from the torque of the ropes themselves, dragging men about violently, uncertain if they would recover themselves; how many times conditions grew better in moments only to be thrust once more into the thick of it, worse than before, could not be counted.

As we went deeper, the storm consumed in full any and all remaining light of day. Not a single ray could break its impenetrable cover, and not could be seen in any direction but what treacherous waters and rains existed when the lightning flashed. And for that then, there was not within the storm but what we had brought with us to get ourselves through. For the storm seemed nearly to ingest all that had been and anything we had once gazed to the horizon hoping for. Not could be seen ahead nor scarcely remember from behind once we were within it. It was a perilous obliteration, threatening imminently to steal our vessel of passage and condemn us evermore to the depths of the sea.

It was then by what will, and what will and light alone we carried with us that ultimately ferried us through. For there was not a breath of abandon amongst us, nor a heart which struck a beat out of turn with its brothers. We were forged then of the same mettle of the seven years past, imbued by what we had each brought to, and given the other in our time: what madness the fellows had woke in me which I shared, what jesting spirit the road had required of me to conjure, what wisdom and faith found amongst my time with the man, I could neither have survived without, nor refrained from giving freely to others *of*, and what passion and pulse and daring for the journey, what love for the adventure the captain had given us all, all swirled round then and seemed to conspire as one: forging some singular unity of such seemingly dissonant things, carving us then of the same firmity, the same strength, the same unquitting resolve— to not be bound or broken or burdened by any, to not be lessened or weakened or made small, but to *rise rise rise!* and be unyielding, unwavering, unfailing and without pause. To fight forth fearlessly through the daunting and the impossible, the constraining and the untamed unto its other side. To be not defeated but find ourselves victorious and made better for having known the fight at all. We sung the same song then amongst ourselves in that storm, radiant, but without sound, harmonious, yet lacking voice, our spirits unwilling to be submerged resonated out immaculate against that peerless hell.

And when at last we sailed beyond the storm in full, the winds began to calm and the seas again grew still, the rains slowed to a shy drizzle and then to not at all, and silence filled the air; *stillness* echoed us round as we broke those first new waters, victorious. For not the claps of thunder nor the whistling winds remained to fill our ears, not the obscuring clouds above, but sailed on smooth we did, into seas of unparalleled clarity and calm.

The surface was glass as went, *new waters, fresh waters untouched,* whose glossy veneer was disturbed only by the bow of our own ship, which felt to slow to a near crawl beyond the turbulence of the storm.

These were not the waters we had known in our voyages around the storm in years past, these were something other. And it was difficult at first to say what. But the very air about us seemed to confirm the thought: it was different than it had been, and the seas which now appeared before us were not quite the same.

From the helm I made my way down to the rail, and then to the bow for a better look at the waters themselves. And as I gazed upon them, their stillness and immaculate surface unparalleled, I noticed something curious— the stars reflected in the water's surface were not the same as those which shown above.

For a moment I gazed upon what celestial visages appeared in those waters before me until I understood. I looked from the water to the sky, from the sky and back again, taking note of the differences until I knew: these stars in the water, *they were the stars of my home sky.*

The constellations which could be perceived in the water's surface were the very ones I had looked upon as boy standing within the meadows, and then later as I laid upon the grass in the clearing of the woods.

At once I shot a look to the captain, who seemed in silence to know what had occurred and that it was my time to go.

And as we stood for that precious moment, in marvelous awe of what we had just achieved: the fresh seas which appeared ahead for the sailing, and the passage back to my home at last arriving, of all that had lead us to them— the wind whipped with one final mighty gust, raising my satchel from where it was slung upon the post and onto the deck, stirring from it the stone which had arrived to me when my journey first began.

From my satchel it tumbled out onto the deck, transformed from one of darkest black, to a stone of deeply translucent red, remarkable in its hew and captivating in its luminance. For it seemed most nearly to be its very own source of light, and yet not without reflecting or responding to the light which permeated through it.

"The stone of the philosopher," said the captain pausing, as I gathered up my satchel and held it in my hand. "That is a mighty treasure, dear Galloway. They say that one who has brought forth such an item shall be bound by not, but know a freedom unending, without encumbrance or constraint. For through purity, they have become true master of their shape and soul."

"We shall see." I said, quickly tucking the stone back into my satchel.

In a hurry I made my way back down to the rail, eager to not lose sight of my home sky amongst those waters.

And as I stood and gazed upon them, prepared in all my being to disembark, I looked to my left at the distance ahead, and spied something curious in the waters which awaited: a vast coastline of untouched land began slowly to grow visible, stretching out, pristine and virgin, and absolutely unfound.

The captain grinned as he noticed it, and I too. "It seems something yet awaits!" I called to him through the distance between us. "Have you passion enough left to encounter it?!" I jested, making play at the time we had each been in the seekings of our own, and prepared myself then to dive forth into the waters which held my home sky.

"Good King Galloway!" he shouted back as I stood with one foot mounting the rail. "What man would I be if I did not?! To lose faith, and thereby fail, at the moment of my life's reckoning? Nay. *NAY!*" he said, "I am not a man of the path that has been laid—"

"—but of the *laying*," I shouted back.

"that is this man's breath full made," he finished. "What worth would there be in losing heart now?"

"None for which I could make amends!" I returned. "Farewell, my very dear friends!" I cried to both the captain and the crew. "You shall each and all be always with me!" and made move then to dive forth from the rail to the waters below.

"Galloway!" cried the captain one last time, stopping me. "For your days here!" he said. "—And then some!" and tossed me the small leather pouch he wore on his belt, containing within it the very last coins he had amassed for the voyage. "You may need them where you're going!" he continued, "Can't imagine we will."

"Thank you," I said to him with earnest feeling. "Thank you, my friend." and stowed the pouch in my satchel.

"You are more than deserving," he replied.

And with a final look of fondness, I waved farewell to the captain and his crew, diving forth into the waters beyond the rail of the ship.

***

Into the waters I plunged and began swimming straight down; into a channel of light which cascaded from the moon of the ocean sky above; down into the stars that shimmered in the deep amongst the black. Down and down and deeper did I go, until slowly the stars which lingered there in the silence below, felt to become the stars which shone there in the stillness above. Deeper and deeper became higher and higher, closer and closer, *nearer and nearer*, until slowly I could perceive the surface of the water they were reflected in and at last broke beyond it.

With a great breath, I emerged from the pool I had descended into as a boy, and again beheld the night sky through the circle of the trees. I climbed out and stood upon its bank, watching as their tops again waved to and fro amongst the stirring of the breeze, seeming then to welcome me home. A silent and eternal praise did my soul there sing to that sky, a holy gratitude of graces become, and mysteries, *known*.

And as my spirit had looked long enough upon those stars to feel that their light would never perish, nor again be lost from me, my feet knew where next needed to be gone, and turned steadily round to begin carrying me home.

Through the thickness of the woods we went, *out*, as had been gone *in*: by the patches of moonlight filtered through the branches above, beyond the brambles and the thickets and the deepness of the dark wood; beyond the place where the forest itself seemed to swallow the path that had first let me in. Out and out and out and out I went, until at last I came to stand beyond the line of trees I had not seen since I was a boy.

I knelt down upon the hilltop and looked out to the great valley of my desolate and lifeless home, broken and marred by foes; with figments of shadow, and sorrows, too great to speak of or behold.

And I did then what only there was left to do, and indeed what only there *could* be done: I dug my hands deep into the earth of that place and began to call forth the very essence of my soul as it had become— from the pits of my being to the peaks of my spirit, I raged; with every vital breath and pulse of heart, from every lesson learned along my way, by each skill practiced and capacity gained, to meet those figments of dark with a light, that would not be dimmed or undone.

Indeed what happened next was not what I would have thought, but I see now was all that could have possibly come. For to dispel the shadows was not by match, or not by match *alone*: not from force of will, where fight meets fight, but with a poise of spirit so surely held— there was no hold for the darkness amongst the light.

The shadows came, one by one, to the hundreds, to the thousandth-and-some— but found themselves to pass through me as I had passed through the storm. What will and light had carried me there through, is what will and light carried them, here out, dissolved and broken apart as they flew through me, dispelled and shattered to the other side. For they found no darkness there within in which to hide.

One by one then were those shadows that had come made banished and gone, *banished and gone!* Until once more the lands of my home were again my own.

***

I rose to my feet and stood, fists clinched and palms to my heart, hands held above my head, body gipped in a victory, impossible; soul struck with a passion, unassailable. And let forth then such a freedom cry of a being unconquerable, of a man who would not permit himself be broken by, or subject to, lost or pushed away, estranged or held in exile evermore— that my home became again as it once was. I cried, *I cried!* such a sound out into the lands of my home that what once was dead began again to know life, that the rivers which had once ceased to flow began again to trickle and then to rage, that the grasses which had once perished, sprouted and began to flourish. I cried until the trees flowered and once more bore leaves, until the air was refreshed and renewed, and the animals who had fled, returned and were safe. I cried until the streets of the village and all the world beyond knew promise once more. I cried until the light of the coming day began at last to break anew.

And all was once more as it should have always been.

***

Looking then to my left as I had as a boy, I again beheld the masters of my lands on their hilltop nearby. For they were outside readying for their morning ceremony. And I realized in that moment that I had come to know many of their words as though they were my very own, that I had tasted many of their wisdoms; for they had been the breath of my own life. I realized I had found what truths existed beyond their teachings they had failed to convey, by the merit of my own being, and by the pain of my own existence, with all of its happenings. And in that moment I felt a great swell of love for those masters and their words, despite their inadequacies.

For it was upon the very path without them, that I found myself, in some sense, led *to* them. And I drew a great love for the earth and the madness and the yearning that paved my way then, as I knew each of them to be much the same— the words of the masters and the days of my own; the wisdoms of their tales, and the happenings of mine; the losses of my life and the seekings beyond were all of themselves the same. As if every great tale they had told in its essence, as if each profound learning they had sought to impart had been glimpsed in the days and nights of my very own being. I knew them then, *I knew their words as though they were my own.* Each syllable earned and stanza striven for, with each great new learning not but the possible effort of mine, and yours, and anyone's days.

It was there then, from those high hills of that lush forest, and those rolling slopes of green, with my passage complete, and my home reclaimed and restored, that I began next to make my way slowly down— beyond the village built along the banks of the river, and the soft groves of the quiet orchards, back down to the cottage which sat amongst the fields and grasses of the meadows in the valley.

***

EPILOGUE

Galloway set down the silver pen and rubbed his eyes. For the first day back upon the lands of his home had been long, and the sun now nearly set. Stacking the pages he had written, he arranged them neatly in a pile and placed them to the side of the desk. Leaning over he opened his satchel and reached inside, producing from it, a gorgeous, translucently red stone.

And looking fondly upon it for a moment, Galloway smiled to himself before placing the stone gently atop the pages he had written and rising from the desk.

Stepping outside he drew a deep breath of the coming night air into his lungs and looked to the sky. "It is done," he said to himself aloud. "It is finally done."

When next I take a journey, he thought, it shall be out into the very world itself. For what wonders amongst it yet await?

And leaning over in that moment, he reached down and began gathering up a small bundle of wood which sat amongst the grasses beyond the cottage walls.

Carrying the wood inside, Galloway knelt before the stone of the hearth and began to build a fire in a shape he had imagined as a boy— with the smaller pieces at its base, up to the largest ones to become the body.

Igniting it gently he watched with a silent wonder, the wood crackling and sparking to life. "How strange a thing it is," he said to himself, the fire dancing in his eyes, "to *be* at all."

And as the fire grew and the flames began to warm and light the room, Galloway rose from the hearth and made his way to the window and looked out, gazing softly upon the meadows and out into the hills beyond, all now veiled in the light of the burgeoning moon.

And there, illuminated faintly in that pale hew, far in the distance of the hills beyond, he could see three figures beginning to make their way slowly down. Three figures he had not seen for far too long a time.

After a great many years of being gone, Galloway, was at last back upon the lands of his home.

END